TALES FROM THE ARABIAN NIGHTS I

Publications from
The Scheherazade Foundation

The Secrets of Scheherazade
An Ordered Experience
Tale of a Lantern & Other Stories
The Elephant & The Tortoise & Other Stories
The Monkey's Fiddle & Other Stories
Ghost of the Violet Well & Other Stories
Many Wise Fools & Other Stories
The Frog Prince & Other Stories
The Three Lemons & Other Stories
The Twelve-Headed Griffin & Other Stories
The Antelope Boy & Other Stories
Why the Fish Laughed & Other Stories
Two Cats & Other Stories
Three Stories
The Twilight of the Gods & Other Stories
The Son of Seven Queens & Other Stories
The Moon Maiden & Other Stories
The Metamorphosis & Other Stories
The Celestial Sisters & Other Stories
Tales from the Arabian Nights I
East of the Sun, West of the Moon & Other Stories
The Well at the End of the World & Other Stories

Tales from the Arabian Nights I

Edited & Introduced by

TAHIR SHAH

The Scheherazade Foundation

The Scheherazade Foundation CIC
85 Great Portland Street
London
W1W 7LT
United Kingdom
www.SF.Charity
info@SF.Charity

First published by The Scheherazade Foundation CIC, 2023

TALES FROM
THE ARABIAN NIGHTS I

The Story of the Fisherman & the Genie
The Arabian Nights
Edited by Kate Douglas Wiggin & Nora A. Smith
Charles Scribner's Sons
1912

The Story of the Magic Horse
Stories from The Arabian Nights
Laurence Housman
Hodder & Stoughton Ltd.
1907

The Arabian Nights Entertainments
The Story of Aladdin; or, The Wonderful Lamp
Anonymous
Rand McNally & Co.
1914

ISBN 978-1-915311-31-3

CONTENTS

Series Introduction

From earliest childhood, I was told stories.

Of course, I was – most children are told stories.

After all, telling children stories is one of the foundations that makes their early experiences a childhood.

But as I think back to the first years of my own life, I find myself reeling from the sheer quantity of stories my infant ears took in.

Whereas other children my age were told stories for amusement, my parents (and the people they associated with) recounted the endless streams of tales for a different reason.

In their opinion, stories – and the ability to tell them – were part of an ancient alchemy… a way of processing complex ideas, of solving problems, and of developing the human mind.

My father, the writer and thinker Idries Shah, believed that folklore was the single most important breakthrough ever developed by the human species. The way he saw it, the rise of stories was as consequential as the development of the languages in which they were told.

He would say that, without stories and storytelling, humanity would never have evolved in the way that it has – and that the folktales, which form a bedrock of ancient societies, are more precious than any physical artefact unearthed on an archaeological dig.

As the years of my own childhood slipped by, I found myself unbothered to work out the hidden layers within treasuries of stories – what my father called 'instruction manuals to the world'. Like everyone else, I simply absorbed the individual tales, delighting in them.

And that's it – the key point, the genius of stories and storytelling.

It's a thing I only grasped in adulthood… something that fascinates me deeply.

In the same way you can jump into a car and drive across the country without giving a second thought to the engine or how it works, you can appreciate stories without understanding the hidden layers and devices that make them what they are.

Stories are all around us.

They're in the TV and movies we so adore, in the video games we play, and of course in the books we read. They're in newspapers and magazines, too; in the conversations we share with old friends, and with new ones. They're on our mobile phones, in aeroplanes, in submarines, and even in our dreams.

Our obsession with, and craving for, stories rests squarely with the way we are so absorbed by them, just as it does with the way we don't need to continually consider how and why they work.

Throughout my life, I've devoted an increasing amount of time to gathering stories from all corners of the world.

It began in my late teens, when I began to criss-cross the continents in a crazed preoccupation with folklore. I developed a first-hand love affair with societies that, over millennia, gave birth to their own astonishing traditions of stories and storytelling.

Most of the time, when reading or listening to stories, we forget that these tales have been shaped through the passage of time. Like pebbles in a river smoothed by rushing waters, they were honed through centuries of telling and retelling.

When I was twelve years old, my father published a masterwork, *World Tales*. The first edition was very large and featured hundreds of original illustrations. The book was unlike any that had come before, for it detailed the provenance and history of each story told.

At bedtime one night, he presented me with an advanced copy. For as long as I could remember, my father had been talking about the project.

Having an actual copy in my hands at last was thrilling beyond words.

Peering down at me sternly, my father said:

'This is far more than a book, Tahir Jan. It's the foundation stone of a great building… a building that *is* human culture. As you grow older, and as you go out into the world, you will understand that the folklores contained between the covers of *World Tales* have brought amusement and educated, and have solved problems when they were needed most of all.'

My father was right.

When I eventually headed out into the wilds of the world for the first time, I discovered the stories contained in *World Tales* for myself, along with a great many more. Just as he said, the stories published in his treasury were the warp and weft threads of society. Stories are the matrix on which culture itself is based – a framework that enables daily life to continue as smoothly as it does.

In this series of books, we have drawn together stories from all over the world. It's a mission begun decades ago by *World Tales*.

Some of the pieces will be known to you, and others will not.

Some will be easy to comprehend, while others will be challenging, or even nonsensical.

I'd now like to note something else…

The Occidental world seems to assume stories must appear in certain regimented ways – presented with a well-defined beginning, a middle, and an end. You know what I mean: the protagonist winning against all odds, and the happy ending to it all.

In the ancient tradition of teaching stories, the kind recounted for an eternity around campfires in the desert and in longhouses deep in the jungle, there's no such standardisation.

Rather, there's usually a hotchpotch of conflicting threads: stories without a straight linear narrative but with an underlying turbulence that gets the reader, or the listener, to sit up and think.

At The Scheherazade Foundation, we are preoccupied with the way we can extract knowledge from stories – either deliberately, or in a less structured way.

We hold the firm opinion that, in order to remove the marrow from the bone stories are best served up in the way as they were passed from one generation to the next throughout human history.

In this series, we have drawn together tales that were gathered in particular during the nineteenth and early twentieth centuries. Spanning a vast range of cultures, they offer an extraordinary glimpse into the societies from which they are drawn – societies that were often changed shortly afterwards by social upheaval, technologies, and war.

Indeed, the fact any of them were recorded at all is a thing of wonder.

Intriguingly, some of the tales will now appear dated because vocabulary and writing styles have altered. But the fact that they seem old-fashioned is of great interest – proof of the way stories are constantly changing and evolving from one era to the next.

Over the last thirty years, I've gathered hundreds of tales on my own journeys, most of them spoken directly into my ears by storytellers and fellow travellers, by wizened old men in the middle of nowhere, and by anyone else good enough to indulge my pleas.

On all those zigzagging adventures, one story sticks out, tantalising me whenever I turn it around my head.

It was called 'The Man Who Turned into a Cat'.

The reason I mention it here is not because it was an especially fine tale, but rather because, from that moment, it affected the way I perceive the world.

It was as though I were a lock and that, by hearing the tale, a key had been slipped into me and turned.

Since first receiving it, I've never been quite the same, my state of consciousness having been flipped inside out.

The fellow traveller who recounted 'The Man Who Turned into a Cat' was lost in shadow, no more than a fragment of his left cheek protruding shyly into the light.

We were sitting on low divans in a teahouse in the ancient Afghan city of Herat.

When the tale had been whispered, I sat there in silence for a long while.

'What have you done to me?' I asked after a long pause.

The fellow traveller offered half a smile.

'*I* didn't do anything,' he replied. 'It's the story that's affected you – a story that I myself first heard when I was a child playing in the orchards of Balkh.'

Peering into the shadow, my eyes widened.

'I don't understand,' I said feebly. 'After all, it's not an especially grand story. There wasn't even a jinn.'

The traveller's mouth eased out from the shadows.

Very slowly, it grinned.

'Tales containing the greatest sustenance for a soul speak in the softest voice,' he said.

Tahir Shah

The Story of the Fisherman &
the Genie

THERE WAS ONCE an aged fisherman who was so poor that he could scarcely earn as much as would maintain himself, his wife, and three children. He went every day to fish betimes in the morning, and imposed it as a law upon himself not to cast his nets above four times a day. He went one morning by moonlight, and coming to the seaside, undressed himself, and cast in his nets.

As he drew them toward the shore, he found them very heavy, and thought he had a good draught of fish, at which he rejoiced; but a moment after, perceiving that instead of fish his net contained nothing but the carcass of an ass, he was much vexed.

When he had mended his nets, which the carcass of the ass had broken in several places, he threw them in a second time; and when he drew them, found a great deal of resistance, which made him think he had taken an abundance of fish; but he found nothing except a basket full of gravel and slime, which grieved him extremely.

'O Fortune!' cried he, with a lamentable tone, 'be not angry with me, nor persecute a wretch who prays thee to spare him. I came hither from my house to seek for my livelihood, and thou pronouncest against me a sentence of death. I have no other trade but this to subsist by, and, notwithstanding all my care, I can scarcely provide what is necessary for my family. But I am to blame to complain of thee; thou takest pleasure to persecute honest people, and advancest those who have no virtue to recommend them.'

Having finished this complaint, he fretfully threw away the basket, and, washing his nets from the slime, cast them a third time, but brought up nothing except stones, shells, and mud. No language can express his disappointment; he was almost distracted. However, when day began to appear, he did not forget to say his prayers like a good Mussulman, and he added to them this petition: 'Lord, thou knowest that I cast my nets only four times a day; I have already drawn them three times, without the least reward for my labour: I am only to cast them once more; I pray thee to render the sea favourable to me, as thou didst to Moses.'

The fisherman, having finished this prayer, cast his nets the fourth time; and when he thought it was proper, drew them as formerly with great difficulty; but instead of fish found nothing in them but a vessel of yellow copper, which, from its weight, seemed not to be empty; and he observed that it was fastened and closed with lead, having the impression of a seal upon it.

This turn of fortune rejoiced him: 'I will sell it,' said he, 'to the founder, and with the money buy a measure of corn.'

He examined the vessel on all sides, and shook it to see if its contents made any noise, but heard nothing. This circumstance, with the impression of the seal upon the cover, made him think it enclosed something precious. To try this, he took a knife and opened it with very little labour. He turned the mouth downward, but nothing came out, which surprised him extremely.

He placed it before him, but while he viewed it attentively, there burst forth a very thick smoke, which obliged him to retire two or three paces back.

The smoke ascended to the clouds, and, extending itself along the sea and upon the shore, formed a great mist, which filled the fisherman with astonishment.

When the smoke was all out of the vessel, it reunited, and became a solid body, of which was formed a genie twice as high as the greatest of giants. At the sight of such a monster the fisherman would fain have fled, but was so frightened that he could not move.

'Solomon,' cried the genie immediately, 'Solomon, the great prophet, pardon, pardon; I will never more oppose your will, I will obey all your commands.'

The fisherman, when he heard these words of the genie, recovered his courage and said to him: 'Thou proud spirit, what is it you say? It is above eighteen hundred years since the prophet Solomon died, and we are now at the end of time. Tell me your history, and how you came to be shut up in this vessel.'

The genie, turning to the fisherman with a fierce look, said: 'Thou must address me with more courtesy; thou art a presumptuous fellow to call me a proud spirit; speak to me more respectfully, or I will kill thee.'

'Ah!' replied the fisherman, 'why should you kill me? Did I not just now set you at liberty, and have you already forgotten my services?'

'No, I remember it,' said the genie, 'but that shall not save thy life: I have only one favour to grant thee.'

'And what is that?' asked the fisherman.

'It is,' answered the genie, 'to give thee thy choice in what manner thou wouldst have me put thee to death.'

'But wherein have I offended you?' demanded the fisherman. 'Is that your reward for the service I have rendered you?'

'I cannot treat thee otherwise,' said the genie; 'and that thou mayest know the reason, hearken to my story.'

'I am one of those rebellious spirits that opposed the will of Solomon, the son of David, and to avenge himself, that monarch sent Asaph, the son of Barakhia, his chief minister, to apprehend me. Asaph seized my person, and brought me by force before his master's throne.

'Solomon commanded me to acknowledge his power, and to submit to his commands. I bravely refused, and told him I would rather expose myself to his resentment, than swear fealty as he required. To punish me, he shut me up in this copper vessel; and that I might not break my prison, he himself stamped upon this leaden cover his seal with the great name of God engraven upon it. He then gave the vessel to one of the genies who had submitted, with orders to throw me into the sea.

'During the first hundred years of my imprisonment, I swore that if anyone should deliver me before the expiration of that period, I would make him rich, even after his death; but that century ran out, and nobody did me the good office.

'During the second, I made an oath that I would open all the treasures of the earth to anyone that might set me at liberty; but with no better success.

'In the third, I promised to make my deliverer a potent monarch, and to grant him every day three requests, of what nature soever they might be; but this century passed as well as the two former, and I continued in prison.

'At last, being angry to find myself a prisoner so long, I swore that if afterwards anyone should deliver me, I would kill him without mercy, and grant him no favour but to choose the manner of his death; and, therefore, since thou hast delivered me today, I give thee that choice.'

This discourse afflicted the fisherman extremely: 'I am very unfortunate,' cried he, 'to come hither to do such a kindness to one that is so ungrateful. I beg you to consider your injustice, and revoke such an unreasonable oath; pardon me, and Heaven will pardon you; if you grant me my life, Heaven will protect you from all attempts against your own.'

'No, thy death is resolved on,' said the genie, 'only choose in what manner thou wilt die.'

The fisherman, perceiving the genie to be resolute, was extremely grieved, not so much for himself, as on account of his three children, and bewailed the misery they must be reduced to by his death. He endeavoured still to appease the genie, and said, 'Alas! Be pleased to take pity on me, in consideration of the service I have done you.'

'I have told thee already,' replied the genie, 'it is for that very reason I must kill thee.'

'That is strange,' said the fisherman, 'are you resolved to reward good with evil? The proverb truly says, "He who does good to one who deserves it not, is always ill-rewarded."'

'Do not lose time,' interrupted the genie; 'all thy chattering shall not divert me from my purpose; make haste, and tell me what kind of death thou preferrest?'

Necessity is the mother of invention. The fisherman bethought himself of a stratagem.

'Since I must die then,' said he to the genie, 'I submit to the will of Heaven; but before I choose the manner of my death, I conjure you, by the great name which was engraven upon the seal of the prophet Solomon, to answer me truly the question I am going to ask you.'

The genie finding himself obliged to a positive answer by this adjuration, trembled, and replied to the fisherman: 'Ask what thou wilt, but make haste.'

The genie having thus promised to speak the truth, the fisherman said to him: 'I wish to know if you were actually in this vessel: dare you swear it by the name of the great God?'

'Yes,' replied the genie, 'I do swear by His great name that I was.'

'In good faith,' answered the fisherman, 'I cannot believe you; the vessel is not capable of holding one of your size, and how should it be possible that your whole body could lie in it?'

'I swear to thee, notwithstanding,' replied the genie, 'that I was there just as you see me here. Is it possible that thou dost not believe me after the solemn oath I have taken?'

'Truly not I,' said the fisherman; 'nor will I believe you, unless you go into the vessel again.'

Upon this the body of the genie dissolved and changed itself into smoke, extending as before upon the seashore; and at last being collected, it began to re-enter the vessel, which it continued to do by a slow and equal motion, till no part remained out; when immediately a voice came forth, which said to the fisherman: 'Well, incredulous fellow, dost thou not believe me now?'

The fisherman, instead of answering the genie, took the cover of lead, and having speedily replaced it on the vessel, 'Genie,' cried he, 'now it is your turn to beg my favour, and to choose which way I shall put you to death; but it is better that I should throw you into the sea, whence I took you: and then I will build a house upon the shore, where I will reside and give notice to all fishermen who come to throw in their nets, to beware of such a wicked genie as you are, who have made an oath to kill him that shall set you at liberty.'

The genie, enraged at these expressions, struggled to free himself; but it was impossible, for the impression of Solomon's seal prevented him. Perceiving that the fisherman had the advantage of him, he thought fit to dissemble his anger. 'Fisherman,' said he, 'take heed you do not what you threaten; for what I spoke to you was only by way of jest.'

'O genie!' replied the fisherman, 'thou who wast but a moment ago the greatest of all genies, and now art the least of them, thy crafty discourse will signify nothing, to the sea thou shalt return. If thou hast been there already so long as thou hast told me, thou mayest very well stay there till the day of judgment. I begged of thee, in God's name, not to take away my life, and thou didst reject my prayers; I am obliged to treat thee in the same manner.'

The genie omitted nothing that he thought likely to prevail with the fisherman: 'Open the vessel,' said he, 'give me my liberty, and I promise to satisfy you to your own content.'

'Thou art a traitor,' replied the fisherman, 'I should deserve to lose my life, if I were such a fool as to trust thee.'

'My good fisherman,' replied the genie, 'I conjure you once more not to be guilty of such cruelty; consider that it is not good to avenge one's self, and that, on the other hand, it is commendable to do good for evil; do not treat me as Imama formerly treated Ateca.'

'And what did Imama to Ateca?' inquired the fisherman.

'Ho!' cried the genie, 'if you have a mind to be informed, open the vessel: do you think that I can be in a humour to relate stories in so strait a prison? I will tell you as many as you please, when you have let me out.'

'No,' said the fisherman, 'I will not let thee out; it is in vain to talk of it; I am just going to throw thee into the bottom of the sea.'

'Hear me one word more,' cried the genie; 'I promise to do you no hurt; nay, far from that, I will show you a way to become exceedingly rich.'

The hope of delivering himself from poverty prevailed with the fisherman.

'I could listen to thee,' said he, 'were there any credit to be given to thy word; swear to me, by the great name of God, that thou wilt faithfully perform what thou promisest, and I will open the vessel; I do not believe thou wilt dare to break such an oath.'

The genie swore to him, upon which the fisherman immediately took off the covering of the vessel. At that instant the smoke ascended, and the genie, having resumed his form, the first thing he did was to kick the vessel into the sea. This action alarmed the fisherman.

'Genie,' said he, 'will not you keep the oath you just now made?'

The genie laughed at his fear, and answered: 'Fisherman, be not afraid, I only did it to divert myself, and to see if you would be alarmed at it; but to convince you that I am in earnest, take your nets and follow me.'

As he spoke these words, he walked before the fisherman, who having taken up his nets, followed him, but with some distrust. They passed by the town, and came to the top of a mountain, from whence they descended into a vast plain, which brought them to a lake that lay betwixt four hills.

When they reached the side of the lake, the genie said to the fisherman: 'Cast in your nets and catch fish.'

The fisherman did not doubt of taking some, because he saw a great number in the water; but he was extremely surprised when he found they were of four colours; white, red, blue, and yellow. He threw in his nets and brought out one of each colour. Having never seen the like before, he could not but admire them, and, judging that he might get a considerable sum for them, he was very joyful.

'Carry those fish,' said the genie to him, 'and present them to your sultan; he will give you more money for them. You may come daily to fish in this lake; but I give you warning not to throw in your nets above once a day, otherwise you will repent.'

Having spoken thus, he struck his foot upon the ground, which opened, and after it had swallowed him up, closed again.

The fisherman, being resolved to follow the genie's advice, forbore casting in his nets a second time, and returned to the town very well satisfied, and making a thousand reflections upon his adventure. He went immediately to the sultan's palace to offer his fish, and his majesty was much surprised when he saw the wonders which the fisherman presented. He took them up one after another, and viewed them with attention; and after having admired them a long time,

'Take those fish,' said he to his vizier, 'and carry them to the cook whom the emperor of the Greeks has sent me. I cannot imagine but that they must be as good as they are beautiful.'

The vizier carried them as he was directed, and delivering them to the cook, said: 'Here are four fish just brought to the sultan; he orders you to dress them.'

He then returned to the sultan, who commanded him to give the fisherman four hundred pieces of gold, which he did accordingly.

The fisherman, who had never seen so much money, could scarcely believe his good fortune, but thought the whole must be a dream, until he found it otherwise, by being able to provide necessaries for his family with the produce of his nets.

As soon as the sultan's cook had cleaned the fish, she put them upon the fire in a frying pan, with oil, and when she thought them fried enough on one side, she turned them upon the other; but, O monstrous prodigy! scarcely were they turned, when the wall of the kitchen divided, and a young lady of wonderful beauty entered from the opening. She held a rod in her hand and was clad in flowered satin, with pendants in her ears, a necklace of large pearls, and bracelets of gold set with rubies.

She moved toward the frying pan, to the great amazement of the cook, and striking one of the fish with the end of the rod, said: 'Fish, fish, are you in your duty?'

The fish having answered nothing, she repeated these words, and then the four fish lifted up their heads, and replied: 'Yes, yes: if you reckon, we reckon; if you pay your debts, we pay ours; if you fly, we overcome, and are content.'

As soon as they had finished these words, the lady overturned the frying-pan and returned into the open part of the wall, which closed immediately, and became as it was before.

The cook was greatly frightened at what had happened, and coming a little to herself went to take up the fish that had fallen on the hearth, but found them blacker than coal and not fit to be carried to the sultan. This grievously troubled her, and she fell to weeping most bitterly.

'Alas!' said she, 'what will become of me? If I tell the sultan what I have seen, I am sure he will not believe me, but will be enraged against me.'

While she was thus bewailing herself, the grand vizier entered, and asked her if the fish were ready. She told him all that had occurred, which we may easily imagine astonished him; but without speaking a word of it to the sultan he invented an excuse that satisfied him, and sending immediately for the fisherman bid him bring four more such fish, for a misfortune had befallen the others, so that they were not fit to be carried to the royal table.

The fisherman, without saying anything of what the genie had told him, told the vizier he had a great way to go for them, in order to excuse himself from bringing them that day, but said that he would certainly bring them on the morrow.

Accordingly, the fisherman went away by night, and coming to the lake, threw in his nets betimes next morning, took four fish like the former, and brought them to the vizier at the hour appointed. The minister took them himself, carried them to the kitchen, and shutting himself up with the cook, she cleaned them and put them on the fire.

When they were fried on one side, and she had turned them upon the other, the kitchen wall again opened, and the same lady came in with the rod in her hand, struck one of the fish, spoke to it as before, and all four gave her the same answer.

After they had spoken to the young lady, she overturned the frying pan with her rod, and retired into the wall. The grand vizier being witness to what had passed,

'This is too wonderful and extraordinary,' said he, 'to be concealed from the sultan; I will inform him of this prodigy.'

The sultan, being much surprised, sent immediately for the fisherman, and said to him: 'Friend, cannot you bring me four more such fish?'

The fisherman replied: 'If your majesty will be pleased to allow me three days, I will do it.'

Having obtained his time, he went to the lake immediately, and at the first throwing in of his net he caught four fish, and brought them directly to the sultan, who was so much the more rejoiced, as he did not expect them so soon, and ordered him four hundred pieces of gold.

As soon as the sultan had the fish, he ordered them to be carried into his closet, with all that was necessary for frying them; and having shut himself up with the vizier, the minister cleaned them, put them into the pan, and when they were fried on one side, turned them upon the other; then the wall of the closet opened, but instead of the young lady, there came out a black, in the habit of a slave, and of a gigantic stature, with a great green staff in his hand.

He advanced toward the pan, and touching one of the fish with his staff, said, with a terrible voice: 'Fish, are you in your duty?'

At these words the fish raised up their heads, and answered: 'Yes, yes; we are; if you reckon, we reckon; if you pay your debts, we pay ours; if you fly, we overcome and are content.'

The fish had no sooner finished these words, than the black threw the pan into the middle of the closet, and reduced them to a coal. Having done this, he retired fiercely, and entering again into the aperture, it closed, and the wall appeared just as it did before.

'After what I have seen,' said the sultan to the vizier, 'it will not be possible for me to be easy; these fish, without doubt, signify something extraordinary.'

He sent for the fisherman, and when he came, said to him: 'Fisherman, the fish you have brought us make me very uneasy; where did you catch them?'

'Sir,' answered he, 'I fished for them in a lake situated betwixt four hills, beyond the mountain that we see from hence.'

'Know'st thou not that lake?' said the sultan to the vizier.

'No,' replied the vizier, 'I never so much as heard of it, although I have for sixty years hunted beyond that mountain.'

The sultan asked the fisherman how far the lake might be from the palace. The fisherman answered it was not above three hours' journey; upon this assurance the sultan commanded all his court to take horse, and the fisherman served them for a guide. They all ascended the mountain, and at the foot of it they saw, to their great surprise, a vast plain that nobody had observed till then, and at last they came to the lake, which they found to be situated betwixt four hills, as the fisherman had described.

The water was so transparent that they observed all the fish to be like those which the fisherman had brought to the palace.

The sultan stood upon the bank of the lake, and after beholding the fish with admiration, demanded of his courtiers if it were possible they had never seen this lake which was within so short a distance of the town. They all answered that they had never so much as heard of it.

'Since you all agree that you never heard of it,' said the sultan, 'and as I am no less astonished than you are at this novelty, I am resolved not to return to my palace till I learn how this lake came here, and why all the fish in it are of four colours.'

Having spoken thus, he ordered his court to encamp; and immediately his pavilion and the tents of his household were planted upon the banks of the lake.

When night came the sultan retired under his pavilion, and spoke to the grand vizier thus:

'Vizier, my mind is uneasy; this lake transported hither, the black that appeared to us in my closet, and the fish that we heard speak; all these things so much excite my curiosity that I cannot resist my impatient desire to have it satisfied. To this end I am resolved to withdraw alone from the camp, and I order you to keep my absence secret: stay in my pavilion, and tomorrow morning, when the emirs and courtiers come to attend my levee, send them away and tell them that I am somewhat indisposed and wish to be alone; and the following days tell them the same thing, till I return.'

The grand vizier endeavoured to divert the sultan from this design; he represented to him the danger to which he might be exposed, and that all his labour might perhaps be in vain; but it was to no purpose; the sultan was resolved. He put on a suit fit for walking and took his cimeter; and as soon as he found that all was quiet in the camp, went out alone, and passed over one of the hills without much difficulty; he found the descent still easier, and when he came to the plain, walked on till the sun arose, and then he saw before him, at a considerable distance, a vast building. He rejoiced at the sight, in hopes of receiving there the information he sought.

When he drew near, he found it was a magnificent palace, or rather a strong castle, of black polished marble, and covered with fine steel, as smooth as glass. Being highly pleased that he had so speedily met with something worthy his curiosity, he stopped before the front of the castle, and considered it with attention.

He then advanced toward the gate, which had two leaves, one of them open; though he might immediately have entered, yet he thought it best to knock. This he did at first softly, and waited for some time; but seeing no one, and supposing he had not been heard, he knocked harder the second time, and after that he knocked again and again, but no one yet appearing, he was exceedingly surprised; for he could not think that a castle in such repair was without inhabitants.

'If there be no one in it,' said he to himself, 'I have nothing to fear; and if it be inhabited, I have wherewith to defend myself.'

At last he entered, and when he came within the porch, he cried: 'Is there no one here to receive a stranger who comes in for some refreshment as he passes by?'

He repeated the same words two or three times; but though he spoke very loud, he was not answered. The silence increased his astonishment: he came into a spacious court, and looked on every side for inhabitants, but discovered none.

Perceiving nobody in the court, he entered the grand halls, which were hung with silk tapestry, the alcoves and sofas covered with stuffs of Mecca, and the porches with the richest stuffs of India. He came afterwards into a superb saloon, in the middle of which was a fountain, with a lion of massy gold at each angle: water issued from the mouths of the four lions, and as it fell, formed diamonds and pearls resembling a jet d'eau, which, springing from the middle of the fountain, rose nearly to the top of a cupola painted in Arabesque.

The castle, on three sides, was encompassed by a garden, with parterres of flowers and shrubbery; and to complete the beauty of the place, an infinite number of birds filled the air with their harmonious notes, and always remained there, nets being spread over the garden, and fastened to the palace to confine them. The sultan walked from apartment to apartment, where he found everything rich and magnificent. Being tired with walking, he sat down in a veranda, which had a view over the garden, reflecting upon what he had seen, when suddenly he heard the voice of one complaining, in lamentable tones. He listened with attention, and heard distinctly these words: 'O fortune! thou who wouldst not suffer me longer to enjoy a happy lot, forbear to persecute me, and by a speedy death put an end to my sorrows. Alas! Is it possible that I am still alive, after so many torments as I have suffered!'

The sultan rose up, advanced toward the place whence he heard the voice, and coming to the door of a great hall, opened it, and saw a handsome young man, richly habited, seated upon a throne raised a little above the ground. Melancholy was painted on his countenance. The sultan drew near and saluted him; the young man returned his salutation, by an inclination of his head, not being able to rise, at the same time saying: 'My lord, I should rise to receive you, but am hindered by sad necessity, and therefore hope you will not be offended.'

'My lord,' replied the sultan, 'I am much obliged to you for having so good an opinion of me: as to the reason of your not rising, whatever your apology be, I heartily accept it. Being drawn hither by your complaints, and afflicted by your grief, I come to offer you my help. I flatter myself that you will relate to me the history of your misfortunes; but inform me first of the meaning of the lake near the palace, where the fish are of four colours; whose castle is this; how you came to be here; and why you are alone.'

Instead of answering these questions, the young man began to weep bitterly.

'How inconstant is fortune!' cried he; 'she takes pleasure to pull down those she has raised. Where are they who enjoy quietly the happiness which they hold of her, and whose day is always clear and serene?'

The sultan, moved with compassion to see him in such a condition, prayed him to relate the cause of his excessive grief.

'Alas! My lord,' replied the young man, 'how is it possible but I should grieve, and my eyes be inexhaustible fountains of tears?'

At these words, lifting up his robe, he showed the sultan that he was a man only from the head to the girdle, and that the other half of his body was black marble.

The sultan was much surprised when he saw the deplorable condition of the young man.

'That which you show me,' said he, 'while it fills me with horror, excites my curiosity, so that I am impatient to hear your history, which, no doubt, must be extraordinary, and I am persuaded that the lake and the fish make some part of it; therefore I conjure you to relate it. You will find some comfort in so doing, since it is certain that the unfortunate find relief in making known their distress.'

'I will not refuse your request,' replied the young man, 'though I cannot comply without renewing my grief. But I give you notice beforehand, to prepare your ears, your mind, and even your eyes, for things which surpass all that the imagination can conceive.'

From: The Arabian Nights

The Story of the Magic Horse

In the land of the Persians there lived in ancient times a king who had three daughters and an only son of such beauty that they drew the eyes of all beholders like moonrise in a clear heaven. Now it was the custom in that country for a great festival to be held at the new year, during which people of all grades, from the highest to the lowest, presented themselves before the king with offerings and salutations.

So it happened that on one of these days there came to the king as he sat in state three sages, masters of their craft, bringing gifts for approval. The first had with him a peacock of gold which was so constructed that at the passing of each hour it beat its wings and uttered a cry.

And the king, having proved it, found the gift acceptable and caused the inventor thereof to be suitably rewarded. The second had made a trumpet so that if placed over the gates of a city it blew a blast against any that sought to enter; and thus was the city held safe from surprise by an enemy. And when the king had found that it possessed that property, he accepted it, bestowing on its maker a rich reward.

But the gift of the third sage, who was an Indian, appeared more prodigious than all, for he had brought with him a horse of ivory and ebony, for which he claimed that, at the will of its owner, or of anyone instructed in the secret, it would rise above the earth and fly, arriving at distant places in a marvellously short space of time.

The king, full of wonder at such a statement, and eager to test it, was in some doubt as to how he might do so, for the Indian was unwilling to part with the secret until secure of the reward which in his own mind he had fixed on.

Now it happened that at a distance of some three leagues from the city there stood a mountain the top of which was clearly discernible to all eyes; so, in order that the Indian's word might be proved, the king, pointing to it, said, 'Go yonder, and bring back to me while I wait the branch of a palm tree which grows at the foot of that mountain; then I shall know that what you tell me is true.'

Instantly the Indian set foot in the stirrup and vaulted upon his charger, and scarcely had he turned a small peg which was set in the pommel of the saddle, when the horse rose lightly into the air and bore him away at wondrous speed amid the shouts of the beholders; and while all were still gazing, amazed at so sudden a vanishing, he reappeared high overhead, bearing the palm branch, and descending into their midst alighted upon the very spot from which he had started, where, prostrating himself, he laid the branch at the king's feet.

The king was so delighted when the wonderful properties of the horse had been thus revealed to him, that, eager to possess it, he bade the Indian name his own reward, declaring that no price could be too great. Then said the sage, 'Since your Majesty so truly appreciates the value of my invention, I do not fear that the reward I ask for will seem too high. Give me in marriage the hand of the fairest of your three daughters, and the horse shall be yours.'

At so arrogant a claim all the courtiers burst into loud laughter; the king alone, consumed with the desire of possessing the wonderful treasure, hesitated as to what answer he should give. Then the king's son, Prince Firouz Shah, seeing his father lend ear to so shameful a proposal, became moved with indignation. Determined to defend his sister's honour and his own, he addressed the king.

'Pardon me, Sire,' said he, 'if I take the liberty of speaking. But how shall it be possible for one of the greatest and most powerful monarchs to ally himself to a mere nobody? I entreat you to consider what is due not to yourself alone but to the high blood of your ancestors and of your children.'

'My son,' replied the king of Persia, 'what you say is very true, so far as it goes; but you do not sufficiently consider the value of so incomparable a marvel as this horse has proved itself to be, or how great would be my chagrin if any other monarch came to possess it. And though I have not yet agreed to the Indian's proposal, I cannot incontinently reject it. But first I must be satisfied that the horse will obey other hands besides those of its inventor, else, though I become its possessor, I may find it useless.'

The Indian, who had stood aside during this discussion, was now full of hope, for he perceived that the king had not altogether rejected his terms, and nothing seemed likelier than that the more he became familiar with the properties of the magic horse the more would he wish to possess it.

When, therefore, the king proposed that the horse should be put to a more independent trial under another rider, the

Indian readily agreed; the more so when the prince himself, relinquishing his apparent opposition, came forward and volunteered for the essay.

The king having consented, the prince mounted, and eager in his design to give his father opportunity for cooler reflection, he did not wait to hear all the Indian's instructions, but turning the peg, as he had seen the other do when first mounting, caused the horse to rise suddenly in the air, and was carried away out of sight in an easterly direction more swiftly than an arrow shot from a bow.

No sooner had the horse and its rider disappeared than the king became greatly concerned for his son's safety; and though the sage could justly excuse himself on the ground that the young prince's impatience had caused him to cut short the instructions which would have ensured his safe return, the king choose to vent upon the Indian the full weight of his displeasure; and cursing the day wherein he had first set eyes on the magic horse, he caused its maker to be thrown into prison, declaring that if the prince did not return within a stated time the life of the other should be forfeit.

The Indian had now good cause to repent of the ambition which had brought him to this extremity, for the prince, of whose opposition to his project he had been thoroughly informed, had only to prolong his absence to involve him in irretrievable ruin. But on the failure of arrogant pretensions the sympathy of the judicious is wasted; let us return therefore to Prince Firouz Shah, whom we left flying through the air with incredible swiftness on the back of the magic steed.

For a time, confident of his skill as a rider and undismayed either by the speed or altitude of his flight, the prince had no wish to return to the palace; but presently the thought of his father's anxiety occurred to him, and being of a tender and considerate disposition he immediately endeavoured to divert his steed from its forward course. This he sought to do by turning in the contrary direction the peg which he had handled when mounting, but to his astonishment the horse responded by rising still higher in the air and flying forward with redoubled swiftness.

Had courage then deserted him, his situation might have become perilous; but preserving his accustomed coolness he began carefully to search for the means by which the speed of the machine might be abated, and before long he perceived under the horse's mane a smaller peg, which he had no sooner touched than he felt himself descending rapidly toward the earth, with a speed that lessened the nearer he came to ground.

As he descended, the daylight in which hitherto he had been travelling faded from view, and he passed within a few minutes from sunset into an obscurity so dense that he could no longer distinguish the nature of his environment, till, as the horse alighted, he perceived beneath him a smooth expanse ending abruptly on all sides at an apparent elevation among the objects surrounding it.

Dismounting he found himself on the roof of a large palace, with marble balustrades dividing it in terraces, and at one side a staircase which led down to the interior. With a spirit ever ready for adventure Prince Firouz Shah immediately descended, groping his way through the darkness till he came to a landing on the further side of which an open door led into a room where a dim light was burning.

The prince paused at the doorway to listen, but all he could hear was the sound of men breathing heavily in their sleep. He pushed the door and entered; and there across an inner threshold he saw black eunuchs lying asleep, each with a drawn sword in his hand. Immediately he guessed that something far more fair must lie beyond; so, undeterred by the danger, he advanced, and stepping lightly across their swords passed through silken hangings into the inner chamber.

Here he perceived, amid surroundings of regal magnificence, a number of couches, one of which stood higher than the rest. Upon each of these a fair damsel lay asleep; but upon that which was raised above its fellows lay a form of such perfect and enchanting beauty that the prince had no will or power to turn away after once beholding it.

Approaching the sleeper softly, he kneeled down and plucked her gently by the sleeve; and immediately the princess – for such if rank and beauty accorded she needs must be – opened to him the depths of her lustrous eyes and gazed in quiet amazement at the princely youth whose handsome looks and reverent demeanour banished at once all thought of alarm.

Now it so happened that a son of the king of India was at that time seeking the hand of the princess in marriage; but her father, the king of Bengal, had rejected him owing to his ferocious and disagreeable aspect. When therefore the princess saw one of royal appearance kneeling before her she supposed he could be no other than the suitor whom she knew only by report, and shedding upon him the light of her regard, 'By Allah,' she said, smiling, 'my father lied in saying that good looks were lacking to thee!'

Prince Firouz Shah, perceiving from these words and the glance which accompanied them, that her disposition towards him was favourable, no longer feared to acquaint her with the plight in which he found himself; while the princess, for her part, listened to the story of his adventures with lively interest, and learned, not without secret satisfaction, that her visitor possessed a rank and dignity equal to her own.

Meanwhile, the maidens who were in attendance on the princess had awakened in dismay to the unaccountable apparition of a fair youth kneeling at the feet of their mistress, and, dreading discovery by the attendants, were all at a loss what to do.

The princess however, seeing that they were awake, called them to her with perfect composure and bade them go instantly and prepare an inner chamber where the prince might sleep and recover from the fatigues of his journey; at the same time she gave orders for a rich banquet to be prepared against the time when he should be ready to partake of it.

Then when her visitor had retired, she arose and began to adorn herself in jewels and rich robes and to anoint her body with fragrance, giving her women no rest till the tale of her mirror contented her; and when all had been done many times over, and the last touch of art added to her loveliness, she sent to inquire whether the prince had yet awaked and were ready to receive her.

Before long the princess herself entered to inquire how he had slept, and being fully assured on that score, she gave orders for the banquet to be served. Everything was done in the greatest magnificence, but the princess was full of apologies, declaring the entertainment unworthy of so distinguished a guest.

'You must pardon me, prince,' she said, 'for receiving you with so little state, and after so hasty a preparation; but the chief of the eunuchs does not enter here without my express permission, and I feared that elsewhere our conversation might be interrupted.'

Prince Firouz Shah was now convinced that the inclinations of the princess corresponded with his own; but though her every word and movement increased the tenderness of his passion, he did not forget the respect due to her rank and virtue.

One of her women attendants however, seeing clearly in what direction matters were tending, and fearing for herself the results of a sudden discovery, withdrew secretly, saying nothing to the rest, and running quickly to the chief of the eunuchs she cried,

'O miserable man, what sorry watch is this that thou hast kept, guarding the king's honour; and who is this man or genie that thou hast admitted to the presence of our mistress? Nay, if the matter be not already past remedy the fault is not thine!'

At these words the eunuch leapt up in alarm, and going secretly he lifted the curtain of the inner chamber, and there beheld at the princess's side a youth of such fair and majestical appearance that he durst not intrude unbidden.

He ran shrieking to the king, and as he went he rent his garments and threw dust upon his head.

'O sire and master,' he cried, 'come quickly and save thy daughter, for there is with her a genie in mortal form and like a king's son to look upon, and if he have not already carried her away, make haste and give orders that he be seized, lest thou become childless.'

The king at once arose and went in great haste and fear to his daughter's palace. There he was met by certain of her women, who, seeing his alarm, said, 'O sire, have no fear for the safety of thy daughter; for this young man is as handsome of heart as of person, and as his conduct is chaste, so also are his intentions honourable.'

Then the king's wrath was cooled somewhat; but since much remained which demanded explanation he drew his sword and advanced with a threatening aspect into the room where his daughter and the prince still sat conversing. Prince Firouz Shah observing the newcomer advance upon him in a warlike attitude, drew his own sword and stood ready for defence; whereupon the king, seeing that the other was the stronger, sheathed his weapon, and with a gesture of salutation addressed him courteously.

'Tell me, fair youth,' he said, 'whether you are man or devil, for though in appearance you are human, how else than by devilry have you come here?'

'Sire,' replied the youth, 'but for the respect that is owing to the father of so fair a daughter, I, who am a son of kings, might resent such an imputation. Be assured, however, that by whatever means I have chosen to arrive, my intentions now are altogether human and honourable; for I have no other or dearer wish than to become your son-in-law through my marriage with this princess in whose eyes it is my happiness to have found favour.'

'What you tell me,' answered the king, 'may be all very true; but it is not the custom for the sons of kings to enter into palaces without the permission of their owners, coming, moreover, unannounced and with no retinue or mark of royalty about them. How, then, shall I convince my people that you are a fit suitor for the hand of my daughter?'

'The proof of honour and kingship,' answered the other, 'does not rest in splendour and retinue alone, though these also would be at my call had I the patience to await their arrival from that too distant country where my father is king. Let it suffice if I shall be able to prove my worth alone and unaided, in such a manner as to satisfy all.'

'Alone and unaided?' said the king; 'how may that be?'

'I will prove it thus,' answered the prince. 'Call out your troops and let them surround this palace; tell them that you have here a stranger, of whom nothing is known, who declares that if you will not yield him the hand of your daughter in marriage he will carry her away from you by force. Bid them use all means to capture and slay me, and if I survive so unequal a contest, judge then whether or not I am fit to become your son-in-law.'

The king immediately accepted the proposal, agreeing to abide by the result; yet was he grieved that a youth of such fair looks and promise should throw away his life in so foolhardy an adventure.

As soon as day dawned he sent for his Vizier and bade him cause all the chiefs of his army to assemble with their troops and companies, till presently there were gathered about the palace forty thousand horsemen and the same number of foot; and the king gave them instructions, saying, 'When the young man of whom I have warned you comes forth and challenges you to battle, then fall upon and slay him, for in no wise must he escape.'

He then led the prince to an open space whence he could see the whole army drawn up in array against him.

'Yonder,' said the king, pointing, 'are those with whom you have to contend; go forth and deal with them as seems best to you.'

'Nay,' answered the prince, 'these are not fair conditions, for yonder I see horsemen as well as foot; how shall I contend against these unless I be mounted?'

The king at once offered him the best horse in his stables, but the prince would not hear of it.

'Is it fair,' he said, 'that I should trust my life under such conditions to a horse that I have never ridden? I will ride no horse but that upon which I came hither.'

'Where is that?' enquired the king.

'If it be where I left it,' answered the prince, 'it is upon the roof of the palace.'

All who heard this answer were filled with laughter and astonishment, for it seemed impossible that a horse could have climbed to so high a roof. Nevertheless the king commanded that search should be made, and there, sure enough, those that were sent found the horse of ebony and ivory standing stiff and motionless.

So though it still seemed to them but a thing for jest and mockery, obeying the king's orders they raised it upon their shoulders, and bearing it to earth carried it forth into the open space before the palace where the king's troops were assembled.

Then Prince Firouz Shah advanced, and leaping upon the horse he cried defiance to the eighty thousand men that stood in battle array against him. And they, on their part, seeing the youth so hardily set on his own destruction, drew sword and couched spear, and came all together to the charge.

The prince waited till they were almost upon him, then turning the peg which stood in the pommel of his saddle he caused the horse to rise suddenly in the air, and all the foremost ranks of the enemy came clashing together beneath him.

At that sight the king and all his court drew a breath of astonishment, and the army staggered and swung about this way and that, striking vainly up at the hoofs of the magic horse as it flew over them.

Then the king, full of dread lest this should indeed be some evil genie that sought to carry his daughter away from him, called to his archers to shoot, but before they could make ready their bows Prince Firouz Shah had given another turn to the peg, and immediately the horse sprang upward and rose higher than the roof of the palace, so that all the arrows fell short and rained destruction on those that were below.

Then the prince called to the king, 'O king of Bengal, have I not now proved myself worthy to be thy son-in-law, and wilt thou not give me the hand of thy daughter in marriage?'

But the king's wrath was very great, for he had been made foolish in the eyes of his people, and panic had broken the ranks of his army and many of them were slain; and by no means would he have for his son-in-law one that possessed such power to throw down the order and establishment of his kingdom.

So he cried back to the prince, saying, 'O vile enchanter, get hence as thou valuest thy life, for if ever thou darest to return and set foot within my dominions thy death and not my daughter shall be thy reward!'

Thus he spoke in his anger, forgetting altogether the promise he had made.

Now it should be known that all this time the princess had been watching the combat from the roof of the palace; and as her fear and anxiety for the prince had in the first instance been great, so now was she overjoyed when she saw him rise superior to the dangers which had threatened him. But as soon as she heard her father's words she became filled with fresh fear lest she and her lover were now to be parted; so as the prince came speeding by upon the magic horse she stretched up her arms to him, crying, 'O master of the flying bird, leave me not desolate, for if thou goest from me now I shall die.'

No sooner did Prince Firouz Shah hear those words than he checked his steed in its flight, and swooping low he bore down over the palace roof, and catching the princess up in his arms placed her upon the saddle before him; and straightway at the pressure of its rider the horse rose under them and carried them away high in air, so that they disappeared forthwith from the eyes of the king and his people.

But as they travelled the day grew hot and the sun burned fiercely upon them; and the prince looking down beheld a green meadow by the side of a lake; so he said, 'O desire of my heart, let us go down into yonder meadow and seek rest and refreshment, and there let us wait till it is evening, so that we may come unperceived to my father's palace; and when I have brought thee thither safely and secretly, then will I make preparation so that thou mayest appear at my father's court in such a manner as befits thy rank.'

So the princess consenting, they went down and sat by the lake and solaced themselves sweetly with love till it was evening. Then they rose up and mounted once more upon the magic horse and came by night to the outskirts of the city where dwelt the king of Persia.

Now in the garden of the summer palace which stood without the walls all was silence and solitude, and coming thither unperceived the king's son led the princess to a pavilion, the door of which lay open, and placing before it the magic horse he bade her stay within and keep watch till his messenger should come to take her to the palace which he would cause to be prepared for her.

Leaving her thus safely sheltered, the prince went into the city to present himself before the king his father; and there he found him in deep mourning and affliction because of his son's absence; and his father seeing him, rose up and embraced him tenderly, rejoicing because of his safe return, and eager to know in what way he had fared.

And the prince said, 'O my father, if it be thy good will and pleasure, I have come back to thee far richer than I went. For I have brought with me the fairest princess that the eyes of love have ever looked upon, and she is the daughter of the king of Bengal; and because of my love for her and the great service which she rendered me when I was a stranger in the midst of enemies, therefore have I no heart or mind or will but to win your consent that I may marry her.'

And when the king heard that, and of all that the princess had done, and of how they had escaped together, he gave his consent willingly, and ordered that a palace should be immediately got ready for her reception that she might on the next day appear before the people in a manner befitting her rank.

Then while preparation was going forward, the prince sought news concerning the sage, for he feared that the king might have slain him

'Do not speak of him,' cried the king. 'Would to Heaven that I had never set eyes on him or his invention, for out of this has arisen all my grief and lamentation. Therefore he now lies in prison awaiting death.'

'Nay,' said the prince 'now surely should he be released and suitably rewarded, seeing that unwittingly he hath been the cause of my fortune; but do not give him my sister in marriage.'

So the king sent and caused the Indian to be brought before him clad in a robe of rank.

And the king said to him, 'Because my son, whom thy vile invention carried away from me, hath returned safe and sound, therefore will I spare thy life. And for the reward of thine ingenuity I give thee this robe of honour; but now take thy horse, wherever it may be, and go, nor ever appear in my sight again. And if thou wilt marry, seek one of thine own rank, but do not aspire to the daughters of kings.'

When the Indian heard that, he dissembled his rage, and bowing himself to the earth departed from the king's presence. And, as he went, everywhere in the palace ran the tale how the king's son had returned upon the magic horse, bringing with him a princess of most marvellous beauty, and how they had alighted in the gardens of the summer palace that lay outside the walls.

Now when this was told him the Indian at once saw his opportunity, and going forth from the city in haste he arrived at the summer palace before the messenger with the appointed retinue which the prince and the king were sending. So coming to the pavilion in the garden he found the princess waiting within, and before the door the horse of ivory and ebony. Then was his heart uplifted for joy, the more so when he perceived how far the damsel exceeded in loveliness all that had been told of her.

Entering the chamber where she sat he kissed the ground at her feet; and she, seeing one that wore a robe of office making obeisance before her, speak to him without fear, saying, 'Who art thou?'

The sage answered, 'O moon of beauty, I am but the dust which lies upon the road by which thou art to travel. Yet I come as a messenger from the king's son who hath sent me to bring thee with all speed to a chamber in the royal palace where he now awaits thee.'

Now the Indian was of a form altogether hideous and abominable. The princess looked at him, therefore, in surprise, saying, 'Could not the king's son find anyone to send to me but thee?'

The sage laughed, for he read the meaning of her words.

'O searcher of hearts,' he said, 'do not wonder that the prince hath sent to thee a man whose looks are unattractive, for because of his love toward thee he is grown exceeding jealous. Were it otherwise, I doubt not that he would have chosen the highest and most honourable in the land; but, being what I am, he has preferred to make me his messenger.'

When the princess heard that, she believed him, and because her impatience to be with her lover was great, she yielded herself willingly into his hands. Then the sage mounted upon the horse and took up the damsel behind him; and having bound her to his girdle for safety, he turned the pin so swiftly that immediately they rose up into the air far above the roof of the palace and in full view of the royal retinue which was even then approaching.

Now because his desire to be with his beloved was so strong, the prince himself had come forth before all others to meet her; and when he saw her thus carried away captive, he uttered a loud cry of lamentation, and stretched out his hands toward her. The cry of her lover reached the ears of the princess, and looking down she saw with wonder his gestures of grief and despair.

So she said to the Indian, 'O slave, why art thou bearing me away from thy lord, disobeying his command?'

The sage answered, 'He is not my lord, nor do I owe him any duty or obedience. May Heaven repay on him all the grief he has brought on me, for I was the maker of this horse on which he won thee, and because he stole it from me I was cast into prison. But now for all my wrongs I will take full payment, and will torture his heart as he hath tortured mine. Be of good cheer, therefore, for doubt not that presently I shall seem a more desirable lover in thine eyes than ever he was.'

On hearing these words the princess was so filled with terror and loathing that she endeavoured to cast herself from the saddle; but the Indian having bound her to his girdle, no present escape from him was possible.

The horse had meanwhile carried them far from the city of the king of Persia, and it was yet an early hour after dawn when they arrived over the land of Kashmir. Assured that he was now safe from pursuit, and perceiving an uninhabited country below him, the Indian caused the horse to descend on the edge of a wood bordered by a stream. Here he made the princess dismount, and was proceeding to force upon her his base and familiar attentions, when the cries raised by the princess drew to that spot a party of horsemen who had been hunting in the neighbourhood.

The leader of the party, who chanced to be no other than the sultan of that country, seeing a fair damsel undergoing ill-treatment from one of brutish and malevolent aspect, rode forward and demanded of the Indian by what right he so used her.

The sage boldly declared that she was his wife and that how he used her was no man's business but his own. The damsel, however, contradicted his assertion with indignation and scorn, and so great were her beauty and the dignity of her bearing that her statement of the case had only to be heard to be believed.

The sultan therefore ordered the Indian to be bound and beaten, and afterwards to be led away to the adjacent city and there cast into the deepest dungeon. As for the princess and magic horse, he caused them to be brought to the palace; and there for the damsel he provided a magnificent apartment with slaves and attendants such as befitted her rank; but the horse, whose properties remained secret, since no other use for it could be discovered, was placed in the royal treasury.

Now though the princess was full of joy over her escape from the Indian, and of gratitude to her deliverer, she could not fail to read in the sultan's manner towards her the spell cast by her beauty. And, in fact, no later than the next day, awakened by sounds throughout the whole city of tumult and rejoicing, and inquiring as to the reason, she was informed that these festivities were the prelude to her own nuptials with the sultan which were to be celebrated that very day before sundown.

At this news her consternation was so great that she immediately swooned away, and remained for a long while speechless. But no sooner had she recovered possession of her faculties than her resolution was formed, and when the sultan entered, as is customary on such occasions, to present his compliments and make inquiries as to her health, she fell into an extravagance of attitude and speech, so artfully contrived that all who beheld her became convinced of her insanity. And the more surely to affect her purpose, and at the same time to relieve her feelings, she made a violent attack upon the sultan's person; nor did she desist until she had brought him to recognize that all hopes for the present consummation of the nuptials were useless.

On the following day also, and upon every succeeding one, the princess showed the same violent symptoms whenever the sultan approached her. It was in vain that all the wisest physicians in the country were summoned into consultation. While some declared that her malady was curable, others, to whose word the princess by her actions lent every possible weight, declared that it was incurable; and in no case was any remedy applied that did not seem immediately to aggravate the disorder.

And here for a while we must leave the princess and return to Prince Firouz Shah, whose affliction no words can describe. Unable to endure the burden of his beloved one's absence in the splendours of his father's palace, or to leave her the victim of fate without an attempt at rescue, he put on the disguise of a travelling dervish, and departing secretly from the Persian court set out into the world to seek for her.

For many months he travelled without clue or tidings to guide him; but as Heaven ever bestows favour on constancy in love, so it led him at last to the land of Kashmir, and to the city of its sultan. Now as he drew near to it by the main road, he fell into conversation with a certain merchant, and inquired of him as to the city and the life and conditions of its inhabitants. And the merchant looked at him in surprise, saying, 'Surely you have come from a far country not to have heard of the strange things which have happened here, for everywhere in these regions and among all the caravans goes the story of the strange maiden, and the ebony horse, and the waiting nuptials.'

Now when the prince heard that, he knew that the end of his wanderings was in sight: so looking upon the city with eyes of gladness, 'Tell me,' he said, 'for I know none of these things.'

So the merchant told him truly all that has here been narrated; and having ended he said, 'O dervish, though you are young, you have in your eyes the light of wisdom; and if you have also in your hands the power of healing, then I tell you that in this city fortune awaits you, for the sultan will give even the half of his kingdom to any man that shall restore health of mind to this damsel.'

Then the king's son felt his heart uplifted within him, howbeit he knew well that the fortune he sought would not be of the sultan's choosing; so parting from the merchant, he put on the robe of a physician, and went and presented himself at the palace.

The sultan was glad at his coming, for though many physicians had promised healing and had all failed, still each new arrival gave him fresh hopes. Now as the sight of a physician seemed ever greatly to increase the princess's malady, the sultan led him to a small closet or balcony, that thence he might look upon her unperceived.

So Prince Firouz Shah, having travelled so many miles in search of her, saw his beloved seated in deep despondency by the side of a fountain; and ever with the tears falling down from her eyes she sighed and sang. Now when he heard her voice and the words, and beheld the soft grief of her countenance, then the prince knew that her disorder was only feigned; and he went forth and said to the sultan, 'This malady is curable; but for the cure something is yet lacking. Let me go in and speak with the damsel alone, and on my life I promise that if all be done according to my requirements, before this time tomorrow the cure shall be accomplished.'

At these words the sultan rejoiced greatly, and he ordered the doors of the princess's chamber to be opened to the physician. So Firouz Shah passed in, and he and his beloved were alone together.

Now because of his grief and wanderings and the growth of his beard, the face of the prince was so changed that the princess did not know him; but seeing one before her in the dress of a physician she rose up in pretended frenzy and began to throw herself about with violence, until from utter exhaustion she fell prostrate. Thereupon the prince drew near, and called her gently by name; and immediately when she heard his voice she knew him, and uttered a loud cry.

Then the king's son put his mouth to her ear and said, 'O temptation of all hearts, now spare my life and have patience, for surely I am come to save thee; but if the sultan learn who I am we are dead, thou and I, because his jealousy is great.'

So she replied, saying, 'O thou that bringest me life, tell me what I shall do?'

The prince said, 'When I depart hence let it appear that I have restored to thee the possession of thy faculties; howbeit the full cure is to come after. Therefore when the sultan comes to thee, be sad and meek and do not repulse him as thou hast done aforetime. Yet have no fear but that I will keep thee safe from him to the last.'

And so saying he left the princess and returned to the sultan, and said to him, 'Go in and see whether the cure be not already at work; but approach not near to her, for though the genie that possessed her is bound he is not yet cast forth: nevertheless tomorrow before noon the remedy shall be complete.'

So the sultan went and found her even as he had been told; and with joy and gratitude he returned to Firouz Shah, saying, 'Truly thou art a healer and the rest are but bunglers and fools. Now, therefore, give orders and all shall be done according to thy will. Doubt not that thy reward shall be great.'

Then the prince said, 'Let the horse of ivory and ebony which was with her at the first be brought forth and set again in the place where it was found, and let the damsel also be brought and put into my hand; and it shall be that when I have set her upon the horse, then the evil genie that held her shall be suddenly loosed, passing from her into that which was aforetime his place of bondage. So shall the remedy be complete, and the princess find joy in her lord before the eyes of all.'

Now when the sultan heard that, the mystery of the ebony horse seemed plain to him, and its use manifest. Therefore he gave orders that with all speed the thing should be done as the physician of the princess required it.

So early on the morrow they brought the horse from the royal treasury, and the princess from her chamber, and carried them to the place where they were first found; and all about, a great crowd of the populace was gathered to behold the sight.

Then Prince Firouz Shah took the princess and set her upon the horse, and leaping into the saddle before her he turned the pin of ascent, and immediately the horse rose with a great sound into the air, and hung above the heads of the affrighted populace. And the king's son leaned down from the saddle and cried in a loud voice, 'O sultan of Kashmir, when you wish to espouse princesses which seek your protection, learn first to obtain their consent.'

And so saying he put the horse to its topmost speed, and like an arrow on the wind he and the princess were borne away, and passed and vanished, and were no more seen in that land.

But in the city of the king of Persia great joy and welcome and thanksgiving awaited them; and there without delay the nuptials were solemnized and through all the country the people rejoiced and feasted for a full month. But because of the grief and affliction that it had caused him the king broke the ebony horse and destroyed its motions.

As for the maker thereof, the sultan of Kashmir caused him to be put to a cruel death: and thus is the story of the sage and his invention brought to a full ending.

From: Stories from The Arabian Nights

The Story of Aladdin; or, The Wonderful Lamp

In one of the large and rich cities of China there once lived a tailor named Mustapha. He was very poor. He could hardly, by his daily labour, maintain himself and his family, which consisted only of his wife and a son.

His son, who was called Aladdin, was a very careless and idle fellow. He was disobedient to his father and mother, and would go out early in the morning and stay out all day, playing in the streets and public places with idle children of his own age.

When he was old enough to learn a trade his father took him into his own shop, and taught him how to use his needle; but all his father's endeavours to keep him to his work were vain, for no sooner was his back turned than the boy was gone for that day. Mustapha chastised him, but Aladdin was incorrigible, and his father, to his great grief, was forced to abandon him to his idleness. He was so much troubled about him, that he fell sick and died in a few months.

Aladdin, who was now no longer restrained by the fear of a father, gave himself over entirely to his idle habits, and was never out of the streets from his companions. This course he followed till he was fifteen years old, without giving his mind to any useful pursuit, or the least reflection on what would become of him. As he was one day playing in the street with his evil associates, according to custom, a stranger passing by stood to observe him.

This stranger was a sorcerer, known as the African magician, as he had been but two days arrived from Africa, his native country.

The African magician, observing in Aladdin's countenance something which assured him that he was a fit boy for his purpose, inquired his name and the history of his companions. When he had learned all he desired to know, he went up to him, and taking him aside from his comrades, said, 'Child, was not your father called Mustapha the tailor?'

'Yes, sir,' answered the boy, 'but he has been dead a long time.'

At these words the African magician threw his arms about Aladdin's neck, and kissed him several times, with tears in his eyes, saying, 'I am your uncle. Your worthy father was my own brother. I knew you at first sight, you are so like him.'

Then he gave Aladdin a handful of small money, saying, 'Go, my son, to your mother. Give my love to her, and tell her that I will visit her tomorrow, that I may see where my good brother lived so long, and ended his days.'

Aladdin ran to his mother, overjoyed at the money his uncle had given him.

'Mother,' said he, 'have I an uncle?'

'No, child,' replied his mother, 'you have no uncle by your father's side or mine.'

'I am just now come,' said Aladdin, 'from a man who says he is my uncle, and my father's brother. He cried, and kissed me, when I told him my father was dead, and gave me money, sending his love to you, and promising to come and pay you a visit, that he may see the house my father lived and died in.'

'Indeed, child,' replied the mother, 'your father had no brother, nor have you an uncle.'

The next day the magician found Aladdin playing in another part of the town, and embracing him as before, put two pieces of gold into his hand, and said to him, 'Carry this, child, to your mother. Tell her that I will come and see her tonight, and bid her get us something for supper. But first show me the house where you live.'

Aladdin showed the African magician the house, and carried the two pieces of gold to his mother, who went out and bought provisions; and considering she wanted various utensils, borrowed them of her neighbours. She spent the whole day in preparing the supper; and at night, when it was ready, said to her son, 'Perhaps the stranger knows not how to find our house; go and bring him, if you meet with him.'

Aladdin was just ready to go, when the magician knocked at the door, and came in loaded with wine and all sorts of fruits, which he brought for a dessert. After he had given what he brought into Aladdin's hands, he saluted his mother, and desired her to show him the place where his brother Mustapha used to sit on the sofa; and when she had so done, he fell down, and kissed it several times, crying out, with tears in his eyes, 'My poor brother! how unhappy am I, not to have come soon enough to give you one last embrace!'

Aladdin's mother desired him to sit down in the same place, but he declined.

'No,' said he, 'I shall not do that; but give me leave to sit opposite to it, that although I see not the master of a family so dear to me, I may at least behold the place where he used to sit.'

When the magician had made choice of a place, and sat down, he began to enter into discourse with Aladdin's mother.

'My good sister,' said he, 'do not be surprised at your never having seen me all the time you have been married to my brother Mustapha of happy memory. I have been forty years absent from this country, which is my native place as well as my late brother's. During that time I have travelled into the Indies, Persia, Arabia, and Syria, and afterwards crossed over into Africa, where I took up my abode in Egypt. At last, as it is natural for a man, I was desirous to see my native country again, and to embrace my dear brother; and finding I had strength enough to undertake so long a journey, I made the necessary preparations, and set out. Nothing ever afflicted me so much as hearing of my brother's death. But God be praised for all things! It is a comfort for me to find, as it were, my brother in a son, who has his most remarkable features.'

The African magician, perceiving that the widow wept at the remembrance of her husband, changed the conversation, and turning toward her son, asked him, 'What business do you follow? Are you of any trade?'

At this question the youth hung down his head, and was not a little abashed when his mother answered, 'Aladdin is an idle fellow. His father, when alive, strove all he could to teach him his trade, but could not succeed; and since his death, notwithstanding all I can say to him, he does nothing but idle away his time in the streets, as you saw him, without considering he is no longer a child; and if you do not make him ashamed of it, I despair of his ever coming to any good. For my part, I am resolved, one of these days, to turn him out of doors, and let him provide for himself.'

After these words, Aladdin's mother burst into tears; and the magician said, 'This is not well, nephew; you must think of helping yourself, and getting your livelihood. There are many sorts of trades; perhaps you do not like your father's, and would prefer another; I will endeavour to help you. If you have no mind to learn any handicraft, I will take a shop for you, furnish it with all sorts of fine stuffs and linens; and then with the money you make of them you can lay in fresh goods, and live in an honourable way. Tell me freely what you think of my proposal; you shall always find me ready to keep my word.'

This plan just suited Aladdin, who hated work. He told the magician he had a greater inclination to that business than to any other, and that he should be much obliged to him for his kindness.

'Well, then,' said the African magician, 'I will carry you with me tomorrow, clothe you as handsomely as the best merchants in the city, and afterwards we will open a shop as I mentioned.'

The widow, after his promise of kindness to her son, no longer doubted that the magician was her husband's brother. She thanked him for his good intentions; and after having exhorted Aladdin to render himself worthy of his uncle's favour, she served up supper, at which they talked of several indifferent matters; and then the magician took his leave and retired.

He came again the next day, as he had promised, and took Aladdin with him to a merchant, who sold all sorts of clothes for different ages and ranks, ready-made, and a variety of fine stuffs, and bade Aladdin choose those he preferred, which he paid for.

When Aladdin found himself so handsomely equipped, he returned his uncle thanks, who thus addressed him: 'As you are soon to be a merchant, it is proper you should frequent these shops, and become acquainted with them.'

He then showed him the largest and finest mosques, carried him to the khans or inns where the merchants and travellers lodged, and afterwards to the sultan's palace, where he had free access; and at last brought him to his own khan, where, meeting with some merchants he had become acquainted with since his arrival, he gave them a treat, to bring them and his pretended nephew acquainted.

This entertainment lasted till night, when Aladdin would have taken leave of his uncle to go home. The magician would not let him go by himself, but conducted him to his mother, who, as soon as she saw him so well dressed, was transported with joy, and bestowed a thousand blessings upon the magician.

Early the next morning the magician called again for Aladdin, and said he would take him to spend that day in the country, and on the next he would purchase the shop. He then led him out at one of the gates of the city, to some magnificent palaces, to each of which belonged beautiful gardens, into which anybody might enter. At every building he came to he asked Aladdin if he did not think it fine; and the youth was ready to answer, when any one presented itself, crying out, 'Here is a finer house, uncle, than any we have yet seen.'

By this artifice the cunning magician led Aladdin some way into the country; and as he meant to carry him farther, to execute his design, pretending to be tired, he took an opportunity to sit down in one of the gardens, on the brink of a fountain of clear water which discharged itself by a lion's mouth of bronze into a basin.

'Come, nephew,' said he, 'you must be weary as well as I. Let us rest ourselves, and we shall be better able to pursue our walk.'

The magician next pulled from his girdle a handkerchief with cakes and fruit, and during this short repast he exhorted his nephew to leave off bad company, and to seek that of wise and prudent men, to improve by their conversation.

'For,' said he, 'you will soon be at man's estate, and you cannot too early begin to imitate their example.'

When they had eaten as much as they liked, they got up, and pursued their walk through gardens separated from one another only by small ditches, which marked out the limits without interrupting the communication; so great was the confidence the inhabitants reposed in each other.

By this means the African magician drew Aladdin insensibly beyond the gardens, and crossed the country, till they nearly reached the mountains.

At last they arrived between two mountains of moderate height and equal size, divided by a narrow valley, where the magician intended to execute the design that had brought him from Africa to China.

'We will go no farther now,' said he to Aladdin. 'I will show you here some extraordinary things, which, when you have seen, you will thank me for; but while I strike a light, gather up all the loose dry sticks you can see, to kindle a fire with.'

Aladdin found so many dried sticks that he soon collected a great heap. The magician presently set them on fire; and when they were in a blaze he threw in some incense, pronouncing several magical words, which Aladdin did not understand.

He had scarcely done so when the earth opened just before the magician, and disclosed a stone with a brass ring fixed in it. Aladdin was so frightened that he would have run away, but the magician caught hold of him, and gave him such a box on the ear that he knocked him down. Aladdin got up trembling, and, with tears in his eyes, said to the magician, 'What have I done, uncle, to be treated in this severe manner?'

'I am your uncle,' answered the magician; 'I supply the place of your father, and you ought to make no reply. But, child,' added he, softening, 'do not be afraid; for I shall not ask anything of you, but that, if you obey me punctually, you will reap the advantages which I intend you. Know, then, that under this stone there is hidden a treasure, destined to be yours, and which will make you richer than the greatest monarch in the world. No person but yourself is permitted to lift this stone, or enter the cave; so you must punctually execute what I may command, for it is a matter of great consequence both to you and to me.'

Aladdin, amazed at all he saw and heard, forgot what was past, and rising said, 'Well, uncle, what is to be done? Command me. I am ready to obey.'

'I am overjoyed, child,' said the African magician, embracing him. 'Take hold of the ring, and lift up that stone.'

'Indeed, uncle,' replied Aladdin, 'I am not strong enough; you must help me.'

'You have no occasion for my assistance,' answered the magician; 'if I help you, we shall be able to do nothing. Take hold of the ring, and lift it up; you will find it will come easily.'

Aladdin did as the magician bade him, raised the stone with ease, and laid it on one side.

When the stone was pulled up there appeared a staircase about three or four feet deep, leading to a door.

'Descend those steps, my son,' said the African magician, 'and open that door. It will lead you into a palace, divided into three great halls. In each of these you will see four large brass cisterns placed on each side, full of gold and silver; but take care you do not meddle with them. Before you enter the first hall, be sure to tuck up your robe, wrap it about you, and then pass through the second into the third without stopping. Above all things, have a care that you do not touch the walls so much as with your clothes; for if you do, you will die instantly. At the end of the third hall you will find a door which opens into a garden planted with fine trees loaded with fruit. Walk directly across the garden to a terrace, where you will see a niche before you, and in that niche a lighted lamp. Take the lamp down and put it out. When you have thrown away the wick and poured out the liquor, put it in your waistband and bring it to me. Do not be afraid that the liquor will spoil your clothes, for it is not oil, and the lamp will be dry as soon as it is thrown out.'

After these words the magician drew a ring off his finger, and put it on one of Aladdin's, saying, 'It is a talisman against all evil, so long as you obey me. Go, therefore, boldly, and we shall both be rich all our lives.'

Aladdin descended the steps, and, opening the door, found the three halls just as the African magician had described. He went through them with all the precaution the fear of death could inspire, crossed the garden without stopping, took down the lamp from the niche, threw out the wick and the liquor, and, as the magician had desired, put it in his waistband.

But as he came down from the terrace, seeing it was perfectly dry, he stopped in the garden to observe the trees, which were loaded with extraordinary fruit of different colours on each tree.

Some bore fruit entirely white, and some clear and transparent as crystal; some pale red, and others deeper; some green, blue, and purple, and others yellow; in short, there was fruit of all colours. The white were pearls; the clear and transparent, diamonds; the deep red, rubies; the paler, ballas rubies; the green, emeralds; the blue, turquoises; the purple, amethysts; and the yellow, sapphires.

Aladdin, ignorant of their value, would have preferred figs, or grapes, or pomegranates; but as he had his uncle's permission, he resolved to gather some of every sort. Having filled the two new purses his uncle had bought for him with his clothes, he wrapped some up in the skirts of his vest, and crammed his bosom as full as it could hold.

Aladdin, having thus loaded himself with riches of which he knew not the value, returned through the three halls with the utmost precaution, and soon arrived at the mouth of the cave, where the African magician awaited him with the utmost impatience.

As soon as Aladdin saw him, he cried out, 'Pray, uncle, lend me your hand, to help me out.'

'Give me the lamp first,' replied the magician; 'it will be troublesome to you.'

'Indeed, uncle,' answered Aladdin, 'I cannot now; but I will as soon as I am up.'

The African magician was determined that he would have the lamp before he would help him up; and Aladdin, who had encumbered himself so much with his fruit that he could not well get at it, refused to give it to him till he was out of the cave. The African magician, provoked at this obstinate refusal, flew into a passion, threw a little of his incense into the fire, and pronounced two magical words, when the stone which had closed the mouth of the staircase moved into its place, with the earth over it in the same manner as it lay at the arrival of the magician and Aladdin.

This action of the magician plainly revealed to Aladdin that he was no uncle of his, but one who designed him evil. The truth was that he had learned from his magic books the secret and the value of this wonderful lamp, the owner of which would be made richer than any earthly ruler, and hence his journey to China.

His art had also told him that he was not permitted to take it himself, but must receive it as a voluntary gift from the hands of another person. Hence he employed young Aladdin, and hoped by a mixture of kindness and authority to make him obedient to his word and will. When he found that his attempt had failed, he set out to return to Africa, but avoided the town, lest any person who had seen him leave in company with Aladdin should make inquiries after the youth.

Aladdin, being suddenly enveloped in darkness, cried, and called out to his uncle to tell him he was ready to give him the lamp. But in vain, since his cries could not be heard.

He descended to the bottom of the steps, with a design to get into the palace, but the door, which was opened before by enchantment, was now shut by the same means. He then redoubled his cries and tears, sat down on the steps without any hopes of ever seeing light again, and in an expectation of passing from the present darkness to a speedy death.

In this great emergency he said, 'There is no strength or power but in the great and high God'; and in joining his hands to pray he rubbed the ring which the magician had put on his finger. Immediately a genie of frightful aspect appeared, and said, 'What wouldst thou have? I am ready to obey thee. I serve him who possesses the ring on thy finger; I, and the other slaves of that ring.'

At another time Aladdin would have been frightened at the sight of so extraordinary a figure, but the danger he was in made him answer without hesitation, 'Whoever thou art, deliver me from this place.'

He had no sooner spoken these words than he found himself on the very spot where the magician had last left him, and no sign of cave or opening, nor disturbance of the earth. Returning thanks to God for being once more in the world, he made the best of his way home.

When he got within his mother's door, joy at seeing her and weakness for want of sustenance made him so faint that he remained for a long time as dead. As soon as he recovered, he related to his mother all that had happened to him, and they were both very vehement in their complaints of the cruel magician.

Aladdin slept very soundly till late the next morning, when the first thing he said to his mother was, that he wanted something to eat, and wished she would give him his breakfast.

'Alas! child,' said she, 'I have not a bit of bread to give you; you ate up all the provisions I had in the house yesterday; but I have a little cotton which I have spun; I will go and sell it, and buy bread and something for our dinner.'

'Mother,' replied Aladdin, 'keep your cotton for another time, and give me the lamp I brought home with me yesterday. I will go and sell it, and the money I shall get for it will serve both for breakfast and dinner, and perhaps supper too.'

Aladdin's mother took the lamp and said to her son, 'Here it is, but it is very dirty. If it were a little cleaner I believe it would bring something more.'

She took some fine sand and water to clean it. But she had no sooner begun to rub it, than in an instant a hideous genie of gigantic size appeared before her, and said to her in a voice of thunder, 'What wouldst thou have? I am ready to obey thee as thy slave, and the slave of all those who have that lamp in their hands; I, and the other slaves of the lamp.'

Aladdin's mother, terrified at the sight of the genie, fainted; when Aladdin, who had seen such a phantom in the cavern, snatched the lamp out of his mother's hand, and said to the genie boldly, 'I am hungry. Bring me something to eat.'

The genie disappeared immediately, and in an instant returned with a large silver tray, holding twelve covered dishes of the same metal, which contained the most delicious viands; six large white bread cakes on two plates, two flagons of wine, and two silver cups. All these he placed upon a carpet and disappeared; this was done before Aladdin's mother recovered from her swoon.

Aladdin had fetched some water, and sprinkled it in her face to recover her. Whether that or the smell of the meat affected her cure, it was not long before she came to herself.

'Mother,' said Aladdin, 'be not afraid. Get up and eat. Here is what will put you in heart, and at the same time satisfy my extreme hunger.'

His mother was much surprised to see the great tray, twelve dishes, six loaves, the two flagons and cups, and to smell the savoury odour which exhaled from the dishes.

'Child,' said she, 'to whom are we obliged for this great plenty and liberality? Has the sultan been made acquainted with our poverty, and had compassion on us?'

'It is no matter, mother,' said Aladdin. 'Let us sit down and eat; for you have almost as much need of a good breakfast as I myself. When we have done, I will tell you.'

Accordingly, both mother and son sat down and ate with the better relish as the table was so well furnished. But all the time Aladdin's mother could not forbear looking at and admiring the tray and dishes, though she could not judge whether they were silver or any other metal, and the novelty more than the value attracted her attention.

The mother and son sat at breakfast till it was dinner time, and then they thought it would be best to put the two meals together. Yet, after this they found they should have enough left for supper, and two meals for the next day.

When Aladdin's mother had taken away and set by what was left, she went and sat down by her son on the sofa, saying, 'I expect now that you will satisfy my impatience, and tell me exactly what passed between the genie and you while I was in a swoon.'

He readily complied with her request.

She was in as great amazement at what her son told her as at the appearance of the genie, and said to him, 'But, son, what have we to do with genies? I never heard that any of my acquaintance had ever seen one. How came that vile genie to address himself to me, and not to you, to whom he had appeared before in the cave?'

'Mother,' answered Aladdin, 'the genie you saw is not the one who appeared to me. If you remember, he that I first saw called himself the slave of the ring on my finger; and this you saw, called himself the slave of the lamp you had in your hand; but I believe you did not hear him, for I think you fainted as soon as he began to speak.'

'What!' cried the mother, 'was your lamp then the occasion of that cursed genie's addressing himself to me rather than to you? Ah! my son, take it out of my sight, and put it where you please. I had rather you would sell it than run the hazard of being frightened to death again by touching it; and if you would take my advice, you would part also with the ring, and not have anything to do with genies, who, as our prophet has told us, are only devils.'

'With your leave, mother,' replied Aladdin, 'I shall now take care how I sell a lamp which may be so serviceable both to you and me. That false and wicked magician would not have undertaken so long a journey to secure this wonderful lamp if he had not known its value to exceed that of gold and silver. And since we have honestly come by it, let us make a profitable use of it, without making any great show and exciting the envy and jealousy of our neighbours. However, since the genies frighten you so much, I will take it out of your sight, and put it where I may find it when I want it. The ring I cannot resolve to part with; for without that you had never seen me again; and though I am alive now, perhaps, if it were gone, I might not be so some moments hence. Therefore I hope you will give me leave to keep it, and to wear it always on my finger.'

Aladdin's mother replied that he might do what he pleased; for her part, she would have nothing to do with genies, and never say anything more about them.

By the next night they had eaten all the provisions the genie had brought; and the next day Aladdin, who could not bear the thought of hunger, putting one of the silver dishes under his vest, went out early to sell it. Addressing himself to a merchant from Nazareth, whom he met in the streets, he took him aside, and pulling out the plate, asked him if he would buy it.

The merchant from Nazareth took the dish, examined it, and as soon as he found that it was good silver, asked Aladdin at how much he valued it.

Aladdin, who had never been used to such traffic, told him he would trust to his judgment and honour. The merchant from Nazareth was somewhat confounded at this plain dealing; and doubting whether Aladdin understood the material or the full value of what he offered to sell, took a piece of gold out of his purse and gave it him, though it was but the sixtieth part of the worth of the plate. Aladdin, taking the money very eagerly, retired with so much haste that the merchant from Nazareth, not content with the exorbitance of his profit, was vexed he had not penetrated into his ignorance, and was going to run after him, to endeavour to get some change out of the piece of gold. But the boy ran so fast, and had got so far, that it would have been impossible to overtake him.

Before Aladdin went home he called at a baker's, bought some cakes of bread, changed his money, and on his return gave the rest to his mother, who went and purchased provisions enough to last them some time. After this manner they lived, until Aladdin had sold the twelve dishes singly, as necessity pressed, to the merchant from Nazareth, for the same money; who, after the first time, durst not offer him less, for fear of losing so good a bargain.

When he had sold the last dish, he had recourse to the tray, which weighed ten times as much as the dishes, and would have carried it to his old purchaser, but that it was too large and cumbersome; therefore he was obliged to bring him home with him to his mother's, where, after the merchant from Nazareth had examined the weight of the tray, he laid down ten pieces of gold, with which Aladdin was very well satisfied.

When all the money was spent, Aladdin had recourse again to the lamp. He took it in his hands, looked for the part where his mother had rubbed it with the sand, and rubbed it also.

The genie immediately appeared, and said, 'What wouldst thou have? I am ready to obey thee as thy slave, and the slave of all those who have that lamp in their hands; I, and the other slaves of the lamp.'

'I am hungry,' said Aladdin. 'Bring me something to eat.'

The genie disappeared, and presently returned with a tray holding the same number of covered dishes as before, set it down, and vanished.

As soon as Aladdin found that their provisions were again expended, he took one of the dishes, and went to look for the merchant from Nazareth. But as he was passing by a goldsmith's shop, the goldsmith perceiving him, called to him, and said, 'My lad, I imagine that you have something to sell to the merchant, whom I often see you visit. Perhaps you do not know that he is the greatest rogue. I will give you the full worth of what you have to sell, or I will direct you to other merchants who will not cheat you.'

This offer induced Aladdin to pull his plate from under his vest and show it to the goldsmith. At first sight he perceived that it was made of the finest silver, and asked if he had sold such as that to the merchant from Nazareth.

When Aladdin told him he had sold him twelve such, for a piece of gold each,

'What a villain!' cried the goldsmith. 'But,' added he, 'my son, what is past cannot be recalled. By showing you the value of this plate, which is of the finest silver we use in our shops, I will let you see how much the merchant from Nazareth has cheated you.'

The goldsmith took a pair of scales, weighed the dish, and assured him that his plate would fetch by weight sixty pieces of gold, which he offered to pay down immediately.

Aladdin thanked him for his fair dealing, and never after went to any other person.

Though Aladdin and his mother had an inexhaustible treasure in their lamp, and might have had whatever they wished for, yet they lived with the same frugality as before, and it may easily be supposed that the money for which Aladdin had sold the dishes and tray was sufficient to maintain them some time.

During this interval, Aladdin frequented the shops of the principal merchants, where they sold cloth of gold and silver, linens, silk stuffs, and jewellery, and, oftentimes joining in their conversation, acquired a knowledge of the world, and a desire to improve himself. By his acquaintance among the jewellers, he came to know that the fruits which he had gathered when he took the lamp were, instead of coloured glass, stones of inestimable value; but he had the prudence not to mention this to anyone, not even to his mother.

One day as Aladdin was walking about the town he heard an order proclaimed, commanding the people to shut up their shops and houses, and keep within doors while the Princess Buddir al Buddoor, the sultan's daughter, went to the bath and returned.

This proclamation inspired Aladdin with eager desire to see the princess's face, which he determined to gratify by placing himself behind the door of the bath, so that he could not fail to see her face.

Aladdin had not long concealed himself before the princess came. She was attended by a great crowd of ladies, slaves, and mutes, who walked on each side and behind her. When she came within three or four paces of the door of the bath, she took off her veil, and gave Aladdin an opportunity of a full view of her face.

The princess was a noted beauty; her eyes were large, lively, and sparkling; her smile bewitching; her nose faultless; her mouth small; her lips vermilion. It is not therefore surprising that Aladdin, who had never before seen such a blaze of charms, was dazzled and enchanted.

After the princess had passed by, and entered the bath, Aladdin quitted his hiding place, and went home. His mother perceived him to be more thoughtful and melancholy than usual, and asked what had happened to make him so, or if he were ill.

He then told his mother all his adventure, and concluded by declaring, 'I love the princess more than I can express, and am resolved that I will ask her in marriage of the sultan.'

Aladdin's mother listened with surprise to what her son told her. When he talked of asking the princess in marriage, she laughed aloud.

'Alas! child,' said she, 'what are you thinking of? You must be mad to talk thus.'

'I assure you, mother,' replied Aladdin, 'that I am not mad, but in my right senses. I foresaw that you would reproach me with folly and extravagance; but I must tell you once more that I am resolved to demand the princess of the sultan in marriage; nor do I despair of success. I have the slaves of the lamp and of the ring to help me, and you know how powerful their aid is. And I have another secret to tell you; those pieces of glass, which I got from the trees in the garden of the subterranean palace, are jewels of inestimable value, and fit for the greatest monarchs. All the precious stones the jewellers have in Bagdad are not to be compared to mine for size or beauty; and I am sure that the offer of them will secure the favour of the sultan. You have a large porcelain dish fit to hold them; fetch it, and let us see how they will look, when we have arranged them according to their different colours.'

Aladdin's mother brought the china dish. Then he took the jewels out of the two purses in which he had kept them, and placed them in order, according to his fancy.

But the brightness and lustre they emitted in the daytime, and the variety of the colours, so dazzled the eyes both of mother and son that they were astonished beyond measure. Aladdin's mother, emboldened by the sight of these rich jewels, and fearful lest her son should be guilty of greater extravagance, complied with his request, and promised to go early the next morning to the palace of the sultan.

Aladdin rose before daybreak, awakened his mother, pressing her to go to the sultan's palace and to get admittance, if possible, before the grand vizier, the other viziers, and the great officers of state went in to take their seats in the divan, where the sultan always attended in person.

Aladdin's mother took the china dish, in which they had put the jewels the day before, wrapped it in two fine napkins, and set forward for the sultan's palace. When she came to the gates the grand vizier, the other viziers, and most distinguished lords of the court were just gone in; but notwithstanding the crowd of people was great, she got into the divan, a spacious hall, the entrance into which was very magnificent.

She placed herself just before the sultan, and the grand vizier and the great lords, who sat in council on his right and left hand. Several causes were called, according to their order, pleaded and adjudged, until the time the divan generally broke up, when the sultan, rising, returned to his apartment, attended by the grand vizier; the other viziers and ministers of state then retired, as also did all those whose business had called them thither.

Aladdin's mother, seeing the sultan retire, and all the people depart, judged rightly that he would not sit again that day, and resolved to go home.

On her arrival she said, with much simplicity, 'Son, I have seen the sultan, and am very well persuaded he has seen me, too, for I placed myself just before him; but he was so much taken up with those who attended on all sides of him that I pitied him, and wondered at his patience.

At last I believe he was heartily tired, for he rose up suddenly, and would not hear a great many who were ready prepared to speak to him, but went away, at which I was well pleased, for indeed I began to lose all patience, and was extremely fatigued with staying so long. But there is no harm done; I will go again tomorrow. Perhaps the sultan may not be so busy.'

The next morning she repaired to the sultan's palace with the present as early as the day before; but when she came there, she found the gates of the divan shut. She went six times afterwards on the days appointed, placed herself always directly before the sultan, but with as little success as the first morning.

On the sixth day, however, after the divan was broken up, when the sultan returned to his own apartment he said to his grand vizier: 'I have for some time observed a certain woman, who attends constantly every day that I give audience, with something wrapped up in a napkin; she always stands up from the beginning to the breaking up of the audience, and effects to place herself just before me. If this woman comes to our next audience, do not fail to call her, that I may hear what she has to say.'

The grand vizier made answer by lowering his hand, and then lifting it up above his head, signifying his willingness to lose it if he failed.

On the next audience day, when Aladdin's mother went to the divan, and placed herself in front of the sultan as usual, the grand vizier immediately called the chief of the macebearers, and pointing to her bade him bring her before the sultan. The old woman at once followed the macebearer, and when she reached the sultan, bowed her head down to the carpet which covered the platform of the throne, and remained in that posture until he bade her rise.

She had no sooner done so, than he said to her, 'Good woman, I have observed you to stand many days from the beginning to the rising of the divan. What business brings you here?'

At these words, Aladdin's mother prostrated herself a second time, and when she arose, said, 'Monarch of monarchs, I beg of you to pardon the boldness of my petition, and to assure me of your pardon and forgiveness.'

'Well,' replied the sultan, 'I will forgive you, be it what it may, and no hurt shall come to you. Speak boldly.'

When Aladdin's mother had taken all these precautions, for fear of the sultan's anger, she told him faithfully the errand on which her son had sent her, and the event which led to his making so bold a request in spite of all her remonstrances.

The sultan hearkened to this discourse without showing the least anger. But before he gave her any answer, he asked her what she had brought tied up in the napkin. She took the china dish which she had set down at the foot of the throne, untied it, and presented it to the sultan.

The sultan's amazement and surprise were inexpressible, when he saw so many large, beautiful, and valuable jewels collected in the dish. He remained for some time lost in admiration. At last, when he had recovered himself, he received the present from Aladdin's mother's hand, saying, 'How rich, how beautiful!'

After he had admired and handled all the jewels one after another, he turned to his grand vizier, and showing him the dish, said, 'Behold, admire, wonder! And confess that your eyes never beheld jewels so rich and beautiful before.'

The vizier was charmed.

'Well,' continued the sultan, 'what sayest thou to such a present? Is it not worthy of the princess my daughter? And ought I not to bestow her on one who values her at so great a price?'

'I cannot but own,' replied the grand vizier, 'that the present is worthy of the princess; but I beg of your majesty to grant me three months before you come to a final resolution. I hope, before that time, my son, whom you have regarded with your favour, will be able to make a nobler present than this Aladdin, who is an entire stranger to your majesty.'

The sultan granted his request, and he said to the old woman, 'Good woman, go home, and tell your son that I agree to the proposal you have made me; but I cannot marry the princess my daughter for three months. At the expiration of that time, come again.'

Aladdin's mother returned home much more gratified than she had expected, and told her son with much joy the condescending answer she had received from the sultan's own mouth; and that she was to come to the divan again that day three months.

At hearing this news, Aladdin thought himself the most happy of all men, and thanked his mother for the pains she had taken in the affair, the good success of which was of so great importance to his peace that he counted every day, week, and even hour as it passed.

When two of the three months were passed, his mother one evening, having no oil in the house, went out to buy some, and found a general rejoicing – the houses dressed with foliage, silks, and carpeting, and everyone striving to show his joy according to his ability. The streets were crowded with officers in habits of ceremony, mounted on horses richly caparisoned, each attended by a great many footmen.

Aladdin's mother asked the oil merchant what was the meaning of all this preparation of public festivity.

'Whence came you, good woman,' said he, 'that you don't know that the grand vizier's son is to marry the Princess Buddir al Buddoor, the sultan's daughter, tonight? She will presently return from the bath; and these officers whom you see are to assist at the cavalcade to the palace, where the ceremony is to be solemnized.'

Aladdin's mother, on hearing this news, ran home very quickly.

'Child,' cried she, 'you are undone! The sultan's fine promises will come to naught. This night the grand vizier's son is to marry the Princess Buddir al Buddoor.'

At this account Aladdin was thunderstruck.

He bethought himself of the lamp, and of the genie who had promised to obey him; and without indulging in idle words against the sultan, the vizier, or his son, he determined, if possible, to prevent the marriage.

When Aladdin had got into his chamber he took the lamp, and rubbing it in the same place as before, immediately the genie appeared, and said to him, 'What wouldst thou have? I am ready to obey thee as thy slave; I, and the other slaves of the lamp.'

'Hear me,' said Aladdin. 'Thou hast hitherto obeyed me, but now I am about to impose on thee a harder task. The sultan's daughter, who was promised me as my bride, is this night married to the son of the grand vizier. Bring them both hither to me immediately they retire to their bedchamber.'

'Master,' replied the genie, 'I obey you.'

Aladdin supped with his mother as was their wont, and then went to his own apartment, and sat up to await the return of the genie, according to his commands.

In the meantime the festivities in honour of the princess's marriage were conducted in the sultan's palace with great magnificence. The ceremonies were at last brought to a conclusion, and the princess and the son of the vizier retired to the bedchamber prepared for them.

No sooner had they entered it, and dismissed their attendants, than the genie, the faithful slave of the lamp, to the great amazement and alarm of the bride and bridegroom took up the bed, and by an agency invisible to them, transported it in an instant into Aladdin's chamber, where he set it down.

'Remove the bridegroom,' said Aladdin to the genie, 'and keep him a prisoner till tomorrow dawn, and then return with him here.'

On Aladdin being left alone with the princess, he endeavoured to assuage her fears, and explained to her the treachery practiced upon him by the sultan her father. He then laid himself down beside her, putting a drawn scimitar between them, to show that he was determined to secure her safety, and to treat her with the utmost possible respect.

At break of day, the genie appeared at the appointed hour, bringing back the bridegroom, whom by breathing upon he had left motionless and entranced at the door of Aladdin's chamber during the night, and at Aladdin's command transported the couch, with the bride and bridegroom on it, by the same invisible agency, into the palace of the sultan.

At the instant that the genie had set down the couch with the bride and bridegroom in their own chamber, the sultan came to the door to offer his good wishes to his daughter. The grand vizier's son, who was almost perished with cold, by standing in his thin undergarment all night, no sooner heard the knocking at the door than he got out of bed, and ran into the robing-chamber, where he had undressed himself the night before.

The sultan, having opened the door, went to the bedside, and kissed the princess on the forehead, but was extremely surprised to see her look so melancholy. She only cast at him a sorrowful look, expressive of great affliction. He suspected there was something extraordinary in this silence, and thereupon went immediately to the sultaness's apartment, told her in what a state he found the princess, and how she had received him.

'Sire,' said the sultaness, 'I will go and see her. She will not receive me in the same manner.'

The princess received her mother with sighs and tears, and signs of deep dejection. At last, upon her pressing on her the duty of telling her all her thoughts, she gave to the sultaness a precise description of all that happened to her during the night; on which the sultaness enjoined on her the necessity of silence and discretion, as no one would give credence to so strange a tale. The grand vizier's son, elated with the honour of being the sultan's son-in-law, kept silence on his part, and the events of the night were not allowed to cast the least gloom on the festivities on the following day, in continued celebration of the royal marriage.

When night came, the bride and bridegroom were again attended to their chamber with the same ceremonies as on the preceding evening. Aladdin, knowing that this would be so, had already given his commands to the genie of the lamp; and no sooner were they alone than their bed was removed in the same mysterious manner as on the preceding evening; and having passed the night in the same unpleasant way, they were in the morning conveyed to the palace of the sultan.

Scarcely had they been replaced in their apartment, when the sultan came to make his compliments to his daughter. The princess could no longer conceal from him the unhappy treatment she had been subjected to, and told him all that had happened, as she had already related it to her mother.

The sultan, on hearing these strange tidings, consulted with the grand vizier; and finding from him that his son had been subjected by an invisible agency to even worse treatment, he determined to declare the marriage cancelled, and all the festivities, which were yet to last for several days, countermanded and terminated.

This sudden change in the mind of the sultan gave rise to various speculations and reports. Nobody but Aladdin knew the secret, and he kept it with the most scrupulous silence. Neither the sultan nor the grand vizier, who had forgotten

Aladdin and his request, had the least thought that he had any hand in the strange adventures that befell the bride and bridegroom.

On the very day that the three months contained in the sultan's promise expired, the mother of Aladdin again went to the palace, and stood in the same place in the divan. The sultan knew her again, and directed his vizier to have her brought before him.

After having prostrated herself, she made answer, in reply to the sultan: 'Sire, I come at the end of three months to ask of you the fulfilment of the promise you made to my son.'

The sultan little thought the request of Aladdin's mother was made to him in earnest, or that he would hear any more of the matter. He therefore took counsel with his vizier, who suggested that the sultan should attach such conditions to the marriage that no one of the humble condition of Aladdin could possibly fulfil.

In accordance with this suggestion of the vizier, the sultan replied to the mother of Aladdin: 'Good woman, it is true sultans ought to abide by their word, and I am ready to keep mine, by making your son happy in marriage with the princess my daughter. But as I cannot marry her without some further proof of your son being able to support her in royal state, you may tell him I will fulfil my promise as soon as he shall send me forty trays of massy gold, full of the same sort of jewels you have already made me a present of, and carried by the like number of black slaves, who shall be led by as many young and handsome white slaves, all dressed magnificently.

On these conditions I am ready to bestow the princess my daughter upon him; therefore, good woman, go and tell him so, and I will wait till you bring me his answer.'

Aladdin's mother prostrated herself a second time before the sultan's throne, and retired. On her way home, she laughed within herself at her son's foolish imagination.

'Where,' said she, 'can he get so many large gold trays, and such precious stones to fill them? It is altogether out of his power, and I believe he will not be much pleased with my embassy this time.'

When she came home, full of these thoughts, she told Aladdin all the circumstances of her interview with the sultan, and the conditions on which he consented to the marriage.

'The sultan expects your answer immediately,' said she; and then added, laughing, 'I believe he may wait long enough!'

'Not so long, mother, as you imagine,' replied Aladdin.

'This demand is a mere trifle, and will prove no bar to my marriage with the princess. I will prepare at once to satisfy his request.'

Aladdin retired to his own apartment and summoned the genie of the lamp, and required him to immediately prepare and present the gift, before the sultan closed his morning audience, according to the terms in which it had been prescribed. The genie professed his obedience to the owner of the lamp, and disappeared.

Within a very short time, a train of forty black slaves, led by the same number of white slaves, appeared opposite the house in which Aladdin lived. Each black slave carried on his head a basin of massy gold, full of pearls, diamonds, rubies, and emeralds.

Aladdin then addressed his mother: 'Madam, pray lose no time; before the sultan and the divan rise, I would have you return to the palace with this present as the dowry demanded for the princess, that he may judge by my diligence and exactness of the ardent and sincere desire I have to procure myself the honour of this alliance.'

As soon as this magnificent procession, with Aladdin's mother at its head, had begun to march from Aladdin's house, the whole city was filled with the crowds of people desirous to see so grand a sight. The graceful bearing, elegant form, and wonderful likeness of each slave; their grave walk at an equal distance from each other, the lustre of their jewelled girdles, and the brilliancy of the aigrettes of precious stones in their turbans, excited the greatest admiration in the spectators.

As they had to pass through several streets to the palace, the whole length of the way was lined with files of spectators. Nothing, indeed, was ever seen so beautiful and brilliant in the sultan's palace, and the richest robes of the emirs of his court were not to be compared to the costly dresses of these slaves, whom they supposed to be kings.

As the sultan, who had been informed of their approach, had given orders for them to be admitted, they met with no obstacle, but went into the divan in regular order, one part turning to the right and the other to the left. After they were all entered, and had formed a semi-circle before the sultan's throne, the black slaves laid the golden trays on the carpet, prostrated themselves, touching the carpet with their foreheads, and at the same time the white slaves did the same. When they rose, the black slaves uncovered the trays, and then all stood with their arms crossed over their breasts.

In the meantime, Aladdin's mother advanced to the foot of the throne, and having prostrated herself, said to the sultan, 'Sire, my son knows this present is much below the notice of Princess Buddir al Buddoor; but hopes, nevertheless, that your majesty will accept of it, and make it agreeable to the princess, and with the greater confidence since he has endeavoured to conform to the conditions you were pleased to impose.'

The sultan, overpowered by the sight of such more than royal magnificence, replied without hesitation to the words of Aladdin's mother: 'Go and tell your son that I wait with open arms to embrace him; and the more haste he makes to come and receive the princess my daughter from my hands, the greater pleasure he will do me.'

As soon as Aladdin's mother had retired, the sultan put an end to the audience. Rising from his throne, he ordered that the princess's attendants should come and carry the trays into their mistress's apartment, whither he went himself to examine them with her at his leisure.

The fourscore slaves were conducted into the palace; and the sultan, telling the princess of their magnificent apparel, ordered them to be brought before her apartment, that she might see through the lattices he had not exaggerated in his account of them.

In the meantime Aladdin's mother reached home, and showed in her air and countenance the good news she brought to her son.

'My son,' said she, 'you may rejoice you are arrived at the height of your desires. The sultan has declared that you shall marry the Princess Buddir al Buddoor. He waits for you with impatience.'

Aladdin, enraptured with this news, made his mother very little reply, but retired to his chamber. There he rubbed his lamp, and the obedient genie appeared.

'Genie,' said Aladdin, 'convey me at once to a bath, and supply me with the richest and most magnificent robe ever worn by a monarch.'

No sooner were the words out of his mouth than the genie rendered him, as well as himself, invisible, and transported him into a hammam of the finest marble of all sorts of colours; where he was undressed, without seeing by whom, in a magnificent and spacious hall. He was then well-rubbed and washed with various scented waters.

After he had passed through several degrees of heat, he came out quite a different man from what he was before. His skin was clear as that of a child, his body lightsome and free; and when he returned into the hall, he found, instead of his own poor raiment, a robe, the magnificence of which astonished him. The genie helped him to dress, and when he had done, transported him back to his own chamber, where he asked him if he had any other commands.

'Yes,' answered Aladdin, 'bring me a charger that surpasses in beauty and goodness the best in the sultan's stables; with a saddle, bridle, and other caparisons to correspond with his value. Furnish also twenty slaves, as richly clothed as those who carried the present to the sultan, to walk by my side and follow me, and twenty more to go before me in two ranks. Besides these, bring my mother six women slaves to attend her, as richly dressed at least as any of the Princess Buddir al Buddoor's, each carrying a complete dress fit for any sultaness. I want also ten thousand pieces of gold in ten purses; go, and make haste.'

As soon as Aladdin had given these orders, the genie disappeared, but presently returned with the horse, the forty slaves, ten of whom carried each a purse containing ten thousand pieces of gold, and six women slaves, each carrying on her head a different dress for Aladdin's mother, wrapped up in a piece of silver tissue, and presented them all to Aladdin.

He presented the six women slaves to his mother, telling her they were her slaves, and that the dresses they had brought were for her use. Of the ten purses Aladdin took four, which he gave to his mother, telling her those were to supply her with necessaries; the other six he left in the hands of the slaves who brought them, with an order to throw them by handfuls among the people as they went to the sultan's palace. The six slaves who carried the purses he ordered likewise to march before him, three on the right hand and three on the left.

When Aladdin had thus prepared himself for his first interview with the sultan, he dismissed the genie, and immediately mounting his charger, began his march, and though he never was on horseback before, appeared with a grace the most experienced horseman might envy. The innumerable concourse of people through whom he passed made the air echo with their acclamations, especially every time the six slaves who carried the purses threw handfuls of gold among the populace.

On Aladdin's arrival at the palace, the sultan was surprised to find him more richly and magnificently robed than he had ever been himself, and was impressed with his good looks and dignity of manner, which were so different from what he expected in the son of one so humble as Aladdin's mother.

He embraced him with all the demonstrations of joy, and when he would have fallen at his feet, held him by the hand, and made him sit near his throne. He shortly after led him, amidst the sounds of trumpets, hautboys, and all kinds of music, to a magnificent entertainment, at which the sultan and Aladdin ate by themselves, and the great lords of the court, according to their rank and dignity, sat at different tables.

After the feast, the sultan sent for the chief cadi, and commanded him to draw up a contract of marriage between the Princess Buddir al Buddoor and Aladdin. When the contract had been drawn, the sultan asked Aladdin if he would stay in the palace and complete the ceremonies of the marriage that day.

'Sire,' said Aladdin, 'though great is my impatience to enter on the honour granted me by your majesty, yet I beg you to permit me first to build a palace worthy to receive the princess your daughter. I pray you to grant me sufficient ground near your palace, and I will have it completed with the utmost expedition.'

The sultan granted Aladdin his request, and again embraced him. After which he took his leave with as much politeness as if he had been bred up and had always lived at court.

Aladdin returned home in the order he had come, amidst the acclamations of the people, who wished him all happiness and prosperity. As soon as he dismounted, he retired to his own chamber, took the lamp, and summoned the genie as usual, who professed his allegiance.

'Genie,' said Aladdin, 'build me a palace fit to receive the Princess Buddir al Buddoor. Let its materials be made of nothing less than porphyry, jasper, agate, lapis lazuli, and the finest marble. Let its walls be massive gold and silver bricks and laid alternately. Let each front contain six windows, and let the lattices of these (except one, which must be left unfinished) be enriched with diamonds, rubies, and emeralds, so that they shall exceed everything of the kind ever seen in the world. Let there be an inner and outer court in front of the palace, and a spacious garden; but above all things, provide a safe treasure house, and fill it with gold and silver. Let there be also kitchens and storehouses, stables full of the finest horses, with their equerries and grooms, and hunting equipage, officers, attendants, and slaves, both men and women, to form a retinue for the princess and myself. Go and execute my wishes.'

When Aladdin gave these commands to the genie, the sun was set.

The next morning at daybreak the genie presented himself, and, having obtained Aladdin's consent, transported him in a moment to the palace he had made. The genie led him through all the apartments, where he found officers and slaves, habited according to their rank and the services to which they were appointed.

The genie then showed him the treasury, which was opened by a treasurer, where Aladdin saw large vases of different sizes, piled up to the top with money, ranged all around the chamber. The genie thence led him to the stables, where were some of the finest horses in the world, and the grooms busy in dressing them; from thence they went to the storehouses, which were filled with all things necessary, both for food and ornament.

When Aladdin had examined every portion of the palace, and particularly the hall with the four-and-twenty windows, and found it far to exceed his fondest expectations, he said, 'Genie, there is one thing wanting: a fine carpet for the princess to walk upon from the sultan's palace to mine. Lay one down immediately.'

The genie disappeared, and Aladdin saw what he desired executed in an instant. The genie then returned, and carried him to his own home.

When the sultan's porters came to open the gates, they were amazed to find what had been an unoccupied garden filled up with a magnificent palace, and a splendid carpet extending to it all the way from the sultan's palace. They told the strange tidings to the grand vizier, who informed the sultan.

'It must be Aladdin's palace,' the sultan exclaimed, 'which I gave him leave to build for my daughter. He has wished to surprise us, and let us see what wonders can be done in only one night.'

Aladdin, on his being conveyed by the genie to his own home, requested his mother to go to the Princess Buddir al Buddoor, and tell her that the palace would be ready for her reception in the evening. She went, attended by her women slaves, in the same order as on the preceding day.

Shortly after her arrival at the princess's apartment the sultan himself came in, and was surprised to find her, whom he knew only as his suppliant at his divan in humble guise, more richly and sumptuously attired than his own daughter. This gave him a higher opinion of Aladdin, who took such care of his mother, and made her share his wealth and honours.

Shortly after her departure, Aladdin, mounting his horse and attended by his retinue of magnificent attendants, left his paternal home forever, and went to the palace in the same pomp as on the day before. Nor did he forget to take with him the wonderful lamp, to which he owed all his good fortune, nor to wear the ring which was given him as a talisman.

The sultan entertained Aladdin with the utmost magnificence, and at night, on the conclusion of the marriage ceremonies, the princess took leave of the sultan her father. Bands of music led the procession, followed by a hundred state ushers, and the like number of black mutes, in two files, with their officers at their head.

Four hundred of the sultan's young pages carried flambeaux on each side, which, together with the illuminations of the sultan's and Aladdin's palaces, made it as light as day. In this order the princess, conveyed in her litter, and accompanied also by Aladdin's mother, carried in a superb litter and attended by her women slaves, proceeded on the carpet which was spread from the sultan's palace to that of Aladdin.

On her arrival Aladdin was ready to receive her at the entrance, and led her into a large hall, illuminated with an infinite number of wax candles, where a noble feast was served up. The dishes were of massy gold, and contained the most delicate viands. The vases, basins, and goblets were gold also, and of exquisite workmanship, and all the other ornaments and embellishments of the hall were answerable to this display.

The princess, dazzled to see so much riches collected in one place, said to Aladdin, 'I thought, prince, that nothing in the world was so beautiful as the sultan my father's palace, but the sight of this hall alone is sufficient to show I was mistaken.'

When the supper was ended, there entered a company of female dancers, who performed, according to the custom of the country, singing at the same time verses in praise of the bride and bridegroom. About midnight Aladdin's mother conducted the bride to the nuptial apartment, and he soon after retired.

The next morning the attendants of Aladdin presented themselves to dress him, and brought him another habit, as rich and magnificent as that worn the day before. He then ordered one of the horses to be got ready, mounted him, and went in the midst of a large troop of slaves to the sultan's palace to entreat him to take a repast in the princess's palace, attended by his grand vizier and all the lords of his court. The sultan consented with pleasure, rose up immediately, and, preceded by the principal officers of his palace, and followed by all the great lords of his court, accompanied Aladdin.

The nearer the sultan approached Aladdin's palace, the more he was struck with its beauty; but when he entered it, when he came into the hall and saw the windows, enriched with diamonds, rubies, emeralds, all large perfect stones, he was completely surprised, and said to his son-in-law, 'This palace is one of the wonders of the world; for where in all the world besides shall we find walls built of massy gold and silver, and diamonds, rubies, and emeralds composing the windows? But what most surprises me is that a hall of this magnificence should be left with one of its windows incomplete and unfinished.'

'Sire,' answered Aladdin, 'the omission was by design, since I wished that you should have the glory of finishing this hall.'

'I take your intention kindly,' said the sultan, 'and will give orders about it immediately.'

After the sultan had finished this magnificent entertainment, provided for him and for his court by Aladdin, he was informed that the jewellers and goldsmiths attended; upon which he returned to the hall, and showed them the window which was unfinished.

'I sent for you,' said he, 'to fit up this window in as great perfection as the rest. Examine them well, and make all the dispatch you can.'

The jewellers and goldsmiths examined the three-and-twenty windows with great attention, and after they had consulted together, to know what each could furnish, they returned, and presented themselves before the sultan, whose principal jeweller, undertaking to speak for the rest, said, 'Sire, we are all willing to exert our utmost care and industry to obey you; but among us all we cannot furnish jewels enough for so great a work.'

'I have more than are necessary,' said the sultan. 'Come to my palace, and you shall choose what may answer your purpose.'

When the sultan returned to his palace he ordered his jewels to be brought out, and the jewellers took a great quantity, particularly those Aladdin had made him a present of, which they soon used, without making any great advance in their work. They came again several times for more, and in a month's time had not finished half their work. In short, they used all the jewels the sultan had, and borrowed of the vizier, but yet the work was not half done.

Aladdin, who knew that all the sultan's endeavours to make this window like the rest were in vain, sent for the jewellers and goldsmiths, and not only commanded them to desist from their work, but ordered them to undo what they had begun, and to carry all their jewels back to the sultan and to the vizier. They undid in a few hours what they had been six weeks about, and retired, leaving Aladdin alone in the hall. He took the lamp, which he carried about him, rubbed it, and presently the genie appeared.

'Genie,' said Aladdin, 'I ordered thee to leave one of the four-and-twenty windows of this hall imperfect, and thou hast executed my commands exactly; now I would have thee make it like the rest.'

The genie immediately disappeared. Aladdin went out of the hall, and returning soon after, found the window, as he wished it to be, like the others.

In the meantime, the jewellers and goldsmiths repaired to the palace, and were introduced into the sultan's presence, where the chief jeweller presented the precious stones which he had brought back. The sultan asked them if Aladdin had given them any reason for so doing, and they answering that he had given them none, he ordered a horse to be brought, which he mounted, and rode to his son-in-law's palace, with some few attendants on foot, to inquire why he had ordered the completion of the window to be stopped.

Aladdin met him at the gate, and without giving any reply to his inquiries conducted him to the grand saloon, where the sultan, to his great surprise, found that the window, which was left imperfect, corresponded exactly with the others. He fancied at first that he was mistaken, and examined the two windows on each side, and afterwards all the four-and-twenty; but when he was convinced that the window which several workmen had been so long about was finished in so short a time, he embraced Aladdin and kissed him between his eyes.

'My son,' said he, 'what a man you are to do such surprising things always in the twinkling of an eye! There is not your fellow in the world; the more I know, the more I admire you.'

The sultan returned to the palace, and after this went frequently to the window to contemplate and admire the wonderful palace of his son-in-law.

Aladdin did not confine himself in his palace, but went with much state, sometimes to one mosque, and sometimes to another, to prayers, or to visit the grand vizier or the principal lords of the court. Every time he went out he caused two slaves, who walked by the side of his horse, to throw handfuls of money among the people as he passed through the streets and squares.

This generosity gained him the love and blessings of the people, and it was common for them to swear by his head. Thus Aladdin, while he paid all respect to the sultan, won by his affable behaviour and liberality the affection of the people.

Aladdin had conducted himself in this manner several years, when the African magician, who had for some years dismissed him from his recollection, determined to inform himself with certainty whether he perished, as he supposed, in the subterranean cave or not.

After he had resorted to a long course of magic ceremonies, and had formed a horoscope by which to ascertain Aladdin's fate, what was his surprise to find the appearances to declare that Aladdin, instead of dying in the cave, had made his escape, and was living in royal splendour by the aid of the genie of the wonderful lamp!

On the very next day the magician set out, and travelled with the utmost haste to the capital of China, where, on his arrival, he took up his lodgings in a khan.

He then quickly learned about the wealth, charities, happiness, and splendid palace of Prince Aladdin. Directly he saw the wonderful fabric, he knew that none but the genies, the slaves of the lamp, could have performed such wonders, and, piqued to the quick at Aladdin's high estate, he returned to the khan.

On his return he had recourse to an operation of geomancy to find out where the lamp was – whether Aladdin carried it about with him, or where he left it. The result of his consultation informed him, to his great joy, that the lamp was in the palace.

'Well,' said he, rubbing his hands in glee, 'I shall have the lamp, and I shall make Aladdin return to his original mean condition.'

The next day the magician learned from the chief superintendent of the khan where he lodged that Aladdin had gone on a hunting expedition which was to last for eight days, of which only three had expired. The magician wanted to know no more. He resolved at once on his plans.

He went to a coppersmith, and asked for a dozen copper lamps; the master of the shop told him he had not so many by him, but if he would have patience till the next day he would have them ready. The magician appointed his time, and desired him to take care that they should be handsome and well-polished.

The next day the magician called for the twelve lamps, paid the man his full price, put them into a basket hanging on his arm, and went directly to Aladdin's palace. As he approached, he began crying,

'Who will exchange old lamps for new?'

And as he went along, a crowd of children collected, who hooted, and thought him, as did all who chanced to be passing by, a madman or a fool to offer to exchange new lamps for old.

The African magician regarded not their scoffs, hootings, or all they could say to him, but still continued crying, 'Who will exchange old lamps for new?'

He repeated this so often, walking backwards and forward in front of the palace, that the princess, who was then in the hall of the four-and-twenty windows, hearing a man cry something, and seeing a great mob crowding about him, sent one of her women slaves to know what he cried.

The slave returned, laughing so heartily that the princess rebuked her.

'Madam,' answered the slave, laughing still, 'who can forbear laughing, to see an old man with a basket on his arm, full of fine new lamps, asking to exchange them for old ones? The children and mob, crowding about him so that he can hardly stir, make all the noise they can in derision of him.'

Another female slave, hearing this, said, 'Now you speak of lamps, I know not whether the princess may have observed it, but there is an old one upon a shelf of the Prince Aladdin's robing room, and whoever owns it will not be sorry to find a new one in its stead. If the princess chooses, she may have the pleasure of trying if this old man is so silly as to give a new lamp for an old one, without taking anything for the exchange.'

The princess, who knew not the value of the lamp and the interest that Aladdin had to keep it safe, entered into the pleasantry and commanded a slave to take it and make the exchange. The slave obeyed, went out of the hall, and no sooner got to the palace gates than he saw the African magician, called to him, and showing him the old lamp, said, 'Give me a new lamp for this.'

The magician never doubted but this was the lamp he wanted. There could be no other such in this palace, where every utensil was gold or silver. He snatched it eagerly out of the slave's hand, and thrusting it as far as he could into his breast, offered him his basket, and bade him choose which he liked best. The slave picked out one and carried it to the princess; but the change was no sooner made than the place rang with the shouts of the children, deriding the magician's folly.

The African magician stayed no longer near the palace, nor cried any more, 'New lamps for old,' but made the best of his way to his khan. His end was answered, and by his silence he got rid of the children and the mob.

As soon as he was out of sight of the two palaces he hastened down the least-frequented streets. Having no more occasion for his lamps or basket, he set all down in a spot where nobody saw him; then going down another street or two, he walked till he came to one of the city gates, and pursuing his way through the suburbs, which were very extensive, at length he reached a lonely spot, where he stopped till the darkness of the night, as the most suitable time for the design he had in contemplation.

When it became quite dark, he pulled the lamp out of his breast and rubbed it. At that summons the genie appeared, and said, 'What wouldst thou have? I am ready to obey thee as thy slave, and the slave of all those who have that lamp in their hands; both I and the other slaves of the lamp.'

'I command thee,' replied the magician, 'to transport me immediately, and the palace which thou and the other slaves of the lamp have built in this city, with all the people in it, to Africa.'

The genie made no reply, but with the assistance of the other genies, the slaves of the lamp, immediately transported him and the palace, entire, to the spot whither he had been desired to convey it.

Early the next morning when the sultan, according to custom, went to contemplate and admire Aladdin's palace, his amazement was unbounded to find that it could nowhere be seen. He could not comprehend how so large a palace, which he had seen plainly every day for some years, should vanish so soon and not leave the least remains behind. In his perplexity he ordered the grand vizier to be sent for with expedition.

The grand vizier, who, in secret, bore no goodwill to Aladdin, intimated his suspicion that the palace was built by magic, and that Aladdin had made his hunting excursion an excuse for the removal of his palace with the same suddenness with which it had been erected. He induced the sultan to send a detachment of his guard, and to have Aladdin seized as a prisoner of state.

On his son-in-law being brought before him, the sultan would not hear a word from him, but ordered him to be put to death. But the decree caused so much discontent among the people, whose affection Aladdin had secured by his largesse and charities, that the sultan, fearful of an insurrection, was obliged to grant him his life.

When Aladdin found himself at liberty, he again addressed the sultan: 'Sire, I pray you to let me know the crime by which I have thus lost the favour of thy countenance.'

'Your crime!' answered the sultan. 'Wretched man, do you not know it? Follow me, and I will show you.'

The sultan then took Aladdin into the apartment from whence he was wont to look at and admire his palace, and said, 'You ought to know where your palace stood; look, mind, and tell me what has become of it.'

Aladdin did so, and being utterly amazed at the loss of his palace, was speechless.

At last recovering himself, he said, 'It is true, I do not see the palace. It is vanished; but I had no concern in its removal. I beg you to give me forty days, and if in that time I cannot restore it, I will offer my head to be disposed of at your pleasure.'

'I give you the time you ask, but at the end of the forty days forget not to present yourself before me.'

Aladdin went out of the sultan's palace in a condition of exceeding humiliation. The lords who had courted him in the days of his splendour now declined to have any communication with him.

For three days he wandered about the city, exciting the wonder and compassion of the multitude by asking everybody he met if they had seen his palace, or could tell him anything of it.

On the third day he wandered into the country, and as he was approaching a river he fell down the bank with so much violence that he rubbed the ring which the magician had given him so hard, by holding on to the rock to save himself, that immediately the same genie appeared whom he had seen in the cave where the magician had left him.

'What wouldst thou have?' said the genie. 'I am ready to obey thee as thy slave, and the slave of all those that have that ring on their finger; both I and the other slaves of the ring.'

Aladdin, agreeably surprised at an offer of help so little expected, replied, 'Genie, show me where the palace I caused to be built now stands, or transport it back where it first stood.'

'Your command,' answered the genie, 'is not wholly in my power; I am only the slave of the ring, and not of the lamp.'

'I command thee, then,' replied Aladdin, 'by the power of the ring, to transport me to the spot where my palace stands, in what part of the world so-ever it may be.'

These words were no sooner out of his mouth than the genie transported him into Africa, to the midst of a large plain, where his palace stood at no great distance from a city, and, placing him exactly under the window of the princess's apartment, left him.

Now it so happened that shortly after Aladdin had been transported by the slave of the ring to the neighbourhood of his palace, that one of the attendants of the Princess Buddir al Buddoor, looking through the window, perceived him and instantly told her mistress. The princess, who could not believe the joyful tidings, hastened herself to the window, and seeing Aladdin, immediately opened it.

The noise of opening the window made Aladdin turn his head that way, and perceiving the princess, he saluted her with an air that expressed his joy.

'To lose no time,' said she to him, 'I have sent to have the private door opened for you; enter, and come up.'

The private door, which was just under the princess's apartment, was soon opened, and Aladdin was conducted up into the chamber. It is impossible to express the joy of both at seeing each other, after so cruel a separation. After embracing and shedding tears of joy, they sat down, and Aladdin said, 'I beg of you, princess, to tell me what is become of an old lamp which stood upon a shelf in my robing chamber.'

'Alas!' answered the princess, 'I was afraid our misfortune might be owing to that lamp; and what grieves me most is that I have been the cause of it. I was foolish enough to exchange the old lamp for a new one, and the next morning I found myself in this unknown country, which I am told is Africa.'

'Princess,' said Aladdin, interrupting her, 'you have explained all by telling me we are in Africa. I desire you only to tell me if you know where the old lamp now is.'

'The African magician carries it carefully wrapped up in his bosom,' said the princess; 'and this I can assure you, because he pulled it out before me, and showed it to me in triumph.'

'Princess,' said Aladdin, 'I think I have found the means to deliver you and to regain possession of the lamp, on which all my prosperity depends. To execute this design, it is necessary for me to go to the town. I shall return by noon, and will then tell you what must be done by you to ensure success. In the meantime, I shall disguise myself, and I beg that the private door may be opened at the first knock.'

When Aladdin was out of the palace, he looked around him on all sides, and perceiving a peasant going into the country, hastened after him. When he had overtaken him, he made a proposal to him to change clothes, which the man agreed to. When they had made the exchange, the countryman went about his business, and Aladdin entered the neighbouring city.

After traversing several streets, he came to that part of the town where the merchants and artisans had their particular streets according to their trades. He went into that of the druggists; and entering one of the largest and best furnished shops, asked the druggist if he had a certain powder, which he named.

The druggist, judging Aladdin by his habit to be very poor, told him he had it, but that it was very dear; upon which Aladdin, penetrating his thoughts, pulled out his purse, and showing him some gold, asked for half a dram of the powder, which the druggist weighed and gave him, telling him the price was a piece of gold. Aladdin put the money into his hand, and hastened to the palace, which he entered at once by the private door.

When he came into the princess's apartment he said to her, 'Princess, you must take your part in the scheme which I propose for our deliverance. You must overcome your aversion for the magician, and assume a most friendly manner toward him, and ask him to oblige you by partaking of an entertainment in your apartments.

Before he leaves, ask him to exchange cups with you, which he, gratified at the honour you do him, will gladly do, when you must give him the cup containing this powder. On drinking it he will instantly fall asleep, and we will obtain the lamp, whose slaves will do all our bidding, and restore us and the palace to the capital of China.'

The princess obeyed to the utmost her husband's instructions. She assumed a look of pleasure on the next visit of the magician, and asked him to an entertainment, which he most willingly accepted. At the close of the evening, during which the princess had tried all she could to please him, she asked him to exchange cups with her, and giving the signal, had the drugged cup brought to her, which she gave to the magician. Out of compliment to the princess he drank it to the very last drop, when he fell back lifeless on the sofa.

The princess, in anticipation of the success of her scheme, had so placed her women from the great hall to the foot of the staircase that the word was no sooner given that the African magician was fallen backwards, than the door was opened, and Aladdin admitted to the hall.

The princess rose from her seat, and ran, overjoyed, to embrace him; but he stopped her, and said, 'Princess, retire to your apartment; and let me be left alone, while I endeavour to transport you back to China as speedily as you were brought from thence.'

When the princess, her women, and slaves were gone out of the hall, Aladdin shut the door, and going directly to the dead body of the magician, opened his vest, took out the lamp, which was carefully wrapped up, and rubbing it, the genie immediately appeared.

'Genie,' said Aladdin, 'I command thee to transport this palace instantly to the place from whence it was brought hither.'

The genie bowed his head in token of obedience, and disappeared. Immediately the palace was transported into

China, and its removal was felt only by two little shocks, the one when it was lifted up, the other when it was set down, and both in a very short interval of time.

On the morning after the restoration of Aladdin's palace the sultan was looking out of his window, mourning over the fate of his daughter, when he thought that he saw the vacancy created by the disappearance of the palace to be again filled up.

On looking more attentively, he was convinced beyond the power of doubt that it was his son-in-law's palace. Joy and gladness succeeded to sorrow and grief. He at once ordered a horse to be saddled, which he mounted that instant, thinking he could not make haste enough to the place.

Aladdin rose that morning by daybreak, put on one of the most magnificent habits his wardrobe afforded, and went up into the hall of the twenty-four windows, from whence he perceived the sultan approaching, and received him at the foot of the great staircase, helping him to dismount.

He led the sultan into the princess's apartment. The happy father embraced her with tears of joy; and the princess, on her side, afforded similar testimonies of her extreme pleasure. After a short interval, devoted to mutual explanations of all that had happened, the sultan restored Aladdin to his favour, and expressed his regret for the apparent harshness with which he had treated him.

'My son,' said he, 'be not displeased at my proceedings against you; they arose from my paternal love, and therefore you ought to forgive the excesses to which it hurried me.'

'Sire,' replied Aladdin, 'I have not the least reason to complain of your conduct, since you did nothing but what your duty required. This infamous magician, the basest of men, was the sole cause of my misfortune.'

The African magician, who was thus twice foiled in his endeavour to rain Aladdin, had a younger brother, who was as skilful a magician as himself and exceeded him in wickedness and hatred of mankind. By mutual agreement they communicated with each other once a year, however widely separate might be their place of residence from each other.

The younger brother, not having received as usual his annual communication, prepared to take a horoscope and ascertain his brother's proceedings. He, as well as his brother, always carried a geomantic square instrument about him; he prepared the sand, cast the points, and drew the figures.

On examining the planetary crystal, he found that his brother was no longer living, but had been poisoned; and by another observation, that he was in the capital of the kingdom of China; also, that the person who had poisoned him was of mean birth, though married to a princess, a sultan's daughter.

When the magician had informed himself of his brother's fate he resolved immediately to avenge his death, and at once departed for China; where, after crossing plains, rivers, mountains, deserts, and a long tract of country without delay, he arrived after incredible fatigues. When he came to the capital of China he took a lodging at a khan. His magic art soon revealed to him that Aladdin was the person who had been the cause of the death of his brother.

He had heard, too, all the persons of repute in the city talking of a woman called Fatima, who was retired from the world, and of the miracles she wrought. As he fancied that this woman might be serviceable to him in the project he had conceived, he made more minute inquiries, and requested to be informed more particularly who that holy woman was, and what sort of miracles she performed.

'What!' said the person whom he addressed, 'have you never seen or heard of her? She is the admiration of the whole town, for her fasting, her austerities, and her exemplary life. Except Mondays and Fridays, she never stirs out of her little cell; and on those days on which she comes into the town she does an infinite deal of good; for there is not a person who is diseased but she puts her hand on him and cures him.'

Having ascertained the place where the hermitage of this holy woman was, the magician went at night, and plunged a poniard into her heart – killed this good woman. In the morning he dyed his face of the same hue as hers, and arraying himself in her garb, taking her veil, the large necklace she wore round her waist, and her stick, went straight to the palace of Aladdin.

As soon as the people saw the holy woman, as they imagined him to be, they presently gathered about him in a great crowd. Some begged his blessing, others kissed his hand, and others, more reserved, kissed only the hem of his garment; while others, suffering from disease, stooped for him to lay his hands upon them; which he did, muttering some words in form of prayer, and, in short, counterfeiting so well that everybody took him for the holy woman. He came at last to the square before Aladdin's palace.

The crowd and the noise were so great that the princess, who was in the hall of the four-and-twenty windows, heard it, and asked what was the matter. One of her women told her it was a great crowd of people collected about the holy woman to be cured of diseases by the imposition of her hands.

The princess, who had long heard of this holy woman, but had never seen her, was very desirous to have some conversation with her. The chief officer perceiving this, told her it was an easy matter to bring the woman to her if she desired and commanded it; and the princess expressing her wishes, he immediately sent four slaves for the pretended holy woman.

As soon as the crowd saw the attendants from the palace, they made way; and the magician, perceiving also that they were coming for him, advanced to meet them, overjoyed to find his plot succeed so well.

'Holy woman,' said one of the slaves, 'the princess wishes to see you, and has sent us for you.'

'The princess does me too great an honour,' replied the false Fatima; 'I am ready to obey her command.' And at the same time he followed the slaves to the palace.

When the pretended Fatima had made his obeisance, the princess said, 'My good mother, I have one thing to request, which you must not refuse me; it is, to stay with me, that you may edify me with your way of living, and that I may learn from your good example.'

'Princess,' said the counterfeit Fatima, 'I beg of you not to ask what I cannot consent to without neglecting my prayers and devotion.'

'That shall be no hindrance to you,' answered the princess; 'I have a great many apartments unoccupied; you shall choose which you like best, and have as much liberty to perform your devotions as if you were in your own cell.'

The magician, who really desired nothing more than to introduce himself into the palace, where it would be a much easier matter for him to execute his designs, did not long excuse himself from accepting the obliging offer which the princess made him.

'Princess,' said he, 'whatever resolution a poor wretched woman as I am may have made to renounce the pomp and grandeur of this world, I dare not presume to oppose the will and commands of so pious and charitable a princess.'

Upon this the princess, rising up, said, 'Come with me. I will show you what vacant apartments I have, that you may make choice of that you like best.'

The magician followed the princess, and of all the apartments she showed him, made choice of that which was the worst, saying that was too good for him, and that he only accepted it to please her.

Afterwards the princess would have brought him back again into the great hall to make him dine with her; but he, considering that he should then be obliged to show his face, which he had always taken care to conceal with Fatima's veil, and fearing that the princess would find out that he was not Fatima, begged of her earnestly to excuse him, telling her that he never ate anything but bread and dried fruits, and desiring to eat that slight repast in his own apartment.

The princess granted his request, saying, 'You may be as free here, good mother, as if you were in your own cell: I will order you a dinner, but remember, I expect you as soon as you have finished your repast.'

After the princess had dined, and the false Fatima had been sent for by one of the attendants, he again waited upon her.

'My good mother,' said the princess, 'I am overjoyed to see so holy a woman as yourself, who will confer a blessing upon this palace. But now I am speaking of the palace, pray how do you like it? And before I show it all to you, tell me first what you think of this hall.'

Upon this question, the counterfeit Fatima surveyed the hall from one end to the other. When he had examined it well, he said to the princess, 'As far as such a solitary being as I am, who am unacquainted with what the world calls beautiful, can judge, this hall is truly admirable; there wants but one thing.'

'What is that, good mother?' demanded the princess; 'tell me, I conjure you. For my part, I always believed, and have heard say, it wanted nothing; but if it does, it shall be supplied.'

'Princess,' said the false Fatima, with great dissimulation, 'forgive me the liberty I have taken; but my opinion is, if it can be of any importance, that if a roc's egg were hung up in the middle of the dome, this hall would have no parallel in the four quarters of the world, and your palace would be the wonder of the universe.'

'My good mother,' said the princess, 'what is a roc, and where may one get an egg?'

'Princess,' replied the pretended Fatima, 'it is a bird of prodigious size, which inhabits the summit of Mount

Caucasus; the architect who built your palace can get you one.'

After the princess had thanked the false Fatima for what she believed her good advice, she conversed with her upon other matters; but she could not forget the roc's egg, which she resolved to request of Aladdin when next he should visit his apartments.

He did so in the course of that evening, and shortly after he entered, the princess thus addressed him: 'I always believed that our palace was the most superb, magnificent, and complete in the world: but I will tell you now what it wants, and that is a roc's egg hung up in the midst of the dome.'

'Princess,' replied Aladdin, 'it is enough that you think it wants such an ornament; you shall see by the diligence which I use in obtaining it, that there is nothing which I would not do for your sake.'

Aladdin left the Princess Buddir al Buddoor that moment, and went up into the hall of four-and-twenty windows, where, pulling out of his bosom the lamp, which after the danger he had been exposed to he always carried about him, he rubbed it; upon which the genie immediately appeared.

'Genie,' said Aladdin, 'I command thee, in the name of this lamp, bring a roc's egg to be hung up in the middle of the dome of the hall of the palace.'

Aladdin had no sooner pronounced these words than the hall shook as if ready to fall; and the genie said, in a loud and terrible voice,

'Is it not enough that I and the other slaves of the lamp have done everything for you, but you, by an unheard-of ingratitude, must command me to bring my master, and hang him up in the midst of this dome? This attempt deserves that you, the princess, and the palace should be immediately reduced to ashes; but you are spared because this request does not come from yourself. Its true author is the brother of the African magician, your enemy whom you have destroyed. He is now in your palace, disguised in the habit of the holy woman Fatima, whom he has murdered; at his suggestion your wife makes this pernicious demand. His design is to kill you; therefore take care of yourself.'

After these words the genie disappeared.

Aladdin resolved at once what to do. He returned to the princess's apartment, and without mentioning a word of what had happened, sat down, and complained of a great pain which had suddenly seized his head. On hearing this, the princess told him how she had invited the holy Fatima to stay with her, and that she was now in the palace; and at the request of the prince, ordered her to be summoned to her at once.

When the pretended Fatima came, Aladdin said, 'Come hither, good mother; I am glad to see you here at so fortunate a time. I am tormented with a violent pain in my head, and request your assistance, and hope you will not refuse me that cure which you impart to afflicted persons.'

So saying, he arose, but held down his head. The counterfeit Fatima advanced toward him, with his hand all the time on a dagger concealed in his girdle under his gown. Observing this, Aladdin snatched the weapon from his hand, pierced him to the heart with his own dagger, and then pushed him down on the floor.

'My dear prince, what have you done?' cried the princess, in surprise. 'You have killed the holy woman!'

'No, my princess,' answered Aladdin, with emotion, 'I have not killed Fatima, but a villain who would have assassinated me, if I had not prevented him. This wicked man,' added he, uncovering his face, 'is the brother of the magician who attempted our ruin. He has strangled the true Fatima, and disguised himself in her clothes with intent to murder me.'

Aladdin then informed her how the genie had told him these facts, and how narrowly she and the palace had escaped destruction through his treacherous suggestion which had led to her request.

Thus was Aladdin delivered from the persecution of the two brothers, who were magicians.

Within a few years the sultan died in a good old age, and as he left no male children, the Princess Buddir al Buddoor succeeded him, and she and Aladdin reigned together many years, and left a numerous and illustrious posterity.

From: The Arabian Nights Entertainments

Finis

Workbooks From The Scheherazade Foundation

We hope that you have enjoyed this collection of stories, gleaned from varying cultural corners of the world, and that you have been entertained by them.

But, have you considered the deeper meanings and interwoven layers that lie hidden beneath the surface?

At The Scheherazade Foundation, we believe that Teaching-Stories contain wisdom, information, and marvels that have the power to transform the way we think, and thereby change our lives.

Employed as a bedrock of culture throughout the centuries – challenging established patterns of thinking, while passing on knowledge and values – tales such as the ones contained in this volume are a rich resource ready and waiting to be mined.

As an aid to help in the perception of less-obvious facets and layers, we have created a series of original Workbooks. Aimed at stimulating thought-provoking discussions and igniting deep reflection, these tools will assist in unlocking the power of Teaching-Stories.

9 781971 912004